THE
PEOPLE'S
NECROMANCER

BOOK ONE OF THE AGE OF MAGIC

REX JAMESON

First Edition (2018)
ISBN (Electronic): 978-0-9989386-2-2
ISBN (Paperback): 978-0-9989386-1-5

To find out when Rex Jameson has a new release, sign up for his email newsletter at https://rex-jameson.com/new-releases-email-list/.

This book is dedicated to Grandpa Rey. You've inspired me in everything from engineering to love of mathematics, history and college football. For better or worse!

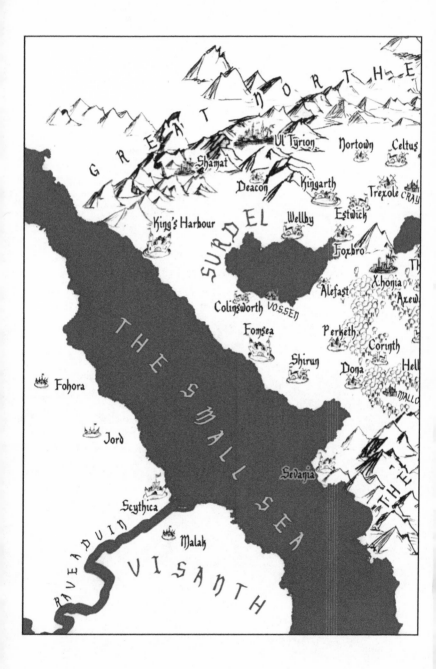

PROLOGUE

THE END OF THE AGE
OF TRANQUILITY

F OR ALMOST 1500 years, the humans in the Kingdom of Surdel managed to live in relative peace, free
from the magics of the great empires to the south
and without conflict from the dark elves in their last ancient
city of Uxmal in the northeast. The monarchs in the family
of Eldenwald still had to contend with civil wars and petty
fights amongst the local nobles. They still had to repel the
frequent invasions by orcish hordes from the southeast. So,
the age had its share of bloodshed and sadness.

The period was not called Tranquility because it lacked
death or conflict. It was called Tranquility because the Kingdom of Surdel was not plagued by what came before when
the dark elves were numerous and aggressive or later when
the mages, the warlocks, and the damned brought madness
to the region.

War may bring death, but magic brings chaos. Dragons bring destruction. The undead bring befoulment. Gods bring combinations of hope, fear, and change.

And the demons? They bring Armageddon.

BIRTH OF A NECROMANCER

ASHTON JERALDSON WAITED outside Clayton's home. Master Nathan had given him the day off. Clayton's day. The funeral. Ashton hadn't knocked on the apartment door. He didn't want to rush Riley. He wouldn't even breathe if it made her uncomfortable. So, he sat, and he waited.

Clayton's parents had decided not to come to the funeral. His father had brought the news to Ashton the day before. Clayton's mother Irma had been too distraught. She didn't want to see the body. She didn't want to watch her son being buried. Clayton's father Earl had decided to stay in Shirun with Irma to comfort her.

Ashton respected their wishes. He would have given anything to not have seen Clayton's body either. Unfortunately, he was there when it happened. Besides, Riley needed Ashton right now like Irma needed Earl back in Shirun. Clayton's body would not be displayed today. He had already been placed in the grave the night before. Today was more of a formal procession and burial service, a tradition of the region.

Riley emerged from her gray home in a simple black dress. No lace. No hat. Her long black hair hung down past her shoulders. Her eyes never left the ground, never acknowledged him. Her face was painted white, as was the custom for widows. Her lips black. Gray around the eyes.

Ashton had never understood the custom. It seemed like a punishment, to paint yourself like the dead you were about to visit. Like a skeleton. He hadn't expected her to look so oddly beautiful though. He wondered if it would be appropriate to tell her, but he thought better of it. Not the right time. Probably never the right time. She was Clayton's wife, the other piece of the puzzle he wasn't connected to anymore.

They didn't talk once during the ten minute walk to the cemetery on the west side of Perketh, but in a way, they still communicated. Their shuffles were in lockstep. He drew immense comfort in the simple act. He wondered if she noticed. He wondered if it helped her like it did him.

When they came to a wall covered in morning glory vines, her legs faltered. He turned to her, confused. Her gray makeup began to drain down her face as her eyes watered. He realized his error in guiding her to this street. It wasn't where Clayton had died, but he and his friend had come here often to find Riley some of her flowers.

"I'll be right back," he said.

He moved along the vines quickly, pressing his face into the flowers like he and Clayton had always done each morning. A certain color strain caught his eye. Dark purple with a pink and white interior. It reminded him of her painted face. He breathed deeply. They smelled fine. He looked back at her as he held the vine that held the purple mutation, seeking her approval.

She smiled, and he felt his heart pump a hundred times faster. He broke three stems without thinking about the need for a variety. He panicked as he looked to her again for approval. She grinned so widely that teeth showed, parting the dark black with pearly whites. His heart slowed to a more appropriate rhythm as he approached her.

"He could have brought me three weeds," she said, "and it still would have brightened my day."

It was Ashton's turn to tear up.

She took the flowers from his hand. She nodded to him, and they resumed their wake across the village. He could smell the morning glories, and his brain flooded with a thousand memories a minute. Clayton and he picking flowers for Riley. Clayton and he skipping rocks across King's Lake. Catching crayfish in the black stream behind the mill. Sitting on the strange, glowing blue rocks in farmer Albertson's fields.

Most of the village turned up for the funeral. Maybe four hundred people. Riley choked up when she saw them. Ashton didn't try to hold her hand. He figured the flowers gave her enough comfort.

He knelt at the foot of the grave. A place of honor. Riley knelt across the grave, behind where Clayton's head laid under the dirt. Hers was the most important position.

Ashton didn't catch a word of the eulogy. He just stared at the dirt mound. Someone had put golden morning glories on Clayton's grave, which wasn't too surprising. Everyone in town knew about their morning ritual.

Riley's black eyeshadow leaked down her face and off her chin, blending in with the black dress. He watched her for a while, a flower as pretty as the morning glories on his friend's grave and just as heartbreaking.

If only he had called out to Clayton sooner. If only they had turned down a different street to hunt for morning glories. Lord Mallory couldn't have possibly gone down every street. There was only the one that headed to Mallory Manor, and Clayton and he had gone down that one because it was so close to the smithy.

He wondered what could have possibly been so important that the Lord had needed to move at such haste. Not that a Lord ever needed a reason. Not that Lord Mallory ever needed to slow down for anyone.

He stared at Riley, and she stared back. He noticed movement in his periphery, but he never evaded her eyes. The villagers were filing out. Mr. Merkins and his brood each patted him on the shoulder. Mrs. Selena. A dozen people he didn't know, probably from the north side where the more affluent lived. People he had played with in nearby fields when he was a kid, some of them from even before he met Clayton, but none of them anywhere near as important to him.

The women filed in line to kiss the widow on the cheek. She didn't acknowledge any of them. She looked like she might fall over at any moment. The females left with black and white makeup on their lips, tokens of the bride of death. She took it as well as could be expected. Dozens bent down to kiss her. Then over a hundred. After an hour, Riley's natural color was showing through the smeared makeup on either cheek.

Eventually, there was no more movement in Ashton's periphery. There was only her and the mound of earth between them. Daylight was waning. She smiled slightly at him before standing up.

"I'm going home," she said.

He nodded. "I'll try to come by later."

He meant it at the time.

She walked past him, back the way they had come from. He looked at the grave and the morning glories that someone had put atop his friend. He pulled one of the glowing blue stones that he and Clayton had collected from Albertson's fields from his pocket. Mr. Albertson claimed they were from leylines, whatever those were. Before Clayton and Ashton began apprenticing under Nathan five years ago at the age of fifteen, they had spent days lounging atop the strange fingers of rock that snaked in and out of the earth. They each had dozens of fragments lining their window sills, believing the stones would bring them luck.

Even though everyone had left, Ashton didn't feel alone. He felt like Clayton was there beside him, hovering over the grave. Ashton wanted so badly to talk to him.

"You weren't supposed to leave me," Ashton said as he placed one stone after another on the grave in a circle around the swath of morning glories. "We made a promise when we were kids. You made me make the promise. Do you remember?"

He completed the circle with an eleventh stone.

"It's not your time," Ashton joked. "You and I are supposed to grow old together. You and Riley are supposed to grow old together. You didn't just make promises to me, Clayton. You made promises to her, too."

He grinned at his old friend through the mound. He imagined Clayton sitting up, wiping the dirt from his face like this had all been a game. "Surprise!" Clayton would say. "I was only fooling!"

Ashton knew this fantasy was silly, but it resembled so many other games they had played together as kids. Hide and seek. Knights and bandits. Playing dead didn't seem so different.

"Come back to us," Ashton said, patting the dirt and smiling to his dead friend. "Come back to your wife. Come back to me."

Daylight retreated across the cemetery. A few stars peaked through the darkening sky.

"Clayton," Ashton said, this time more forcefully. "I can't do this by myself. I'm a shit blacksmith. Master Nathan needs iron spikes that are straight. Horses can't walk with the shoes I give 'em. The town needs you more than it needs me. You can't die here. You hear me?"

Tears welled at the corners of his eyes.

"You hear me, Clayton?!" he yelled into the dirt, his hands flat on the mound.

He imagined his friend's face directly underneath him as he peered into the ground.

"Sit up!" Ashton commanded. "Your wife needs you! I need you!"

The breeze must have picked up because he felt tall grass brushing against him, tickling his chest and sides. He brushed against the weeds but felt something solid and gritty squirming against his hand.

He scrambled backward, gawking at the mound. The circle of stones had been broken and the morning glories disturbed. Ashton's mouth gaped as the confusion ebbed away into realization. There was no tall grass in the cemetery. There had been nothing next to the grave of his friend Clayton. He hadn't imagined the sensation. He had just misinterpreted the source.

Something groped within the darkness. A hand protruding from the freshly dug grave. It pushed the morning glories aside and clawed and pushed the earth.

Ashton scrambled backward until he found his feet. He ran as fast as he could. Down the same road that Lord Mallory had run over his friend. South and then southeast. Through farmer Albertson's fields and over the leyline veins. Past the cows and horses. Through the manicured lines of barley. He ran hard and fast until his legs could move no longer. He crawled into a stranger's barn, miles away from the village of Perketh. His throat was so parched that he happily lapped water from a pig trough. When he had his fill, he crashed face first into the hay beside a fat sow feeding a dozen piglets.

He dreamt of days spent with his friend Clayton in farmer Albertson's fields. He dreamt of picking flowers for Riley. He didn't dream of cemeteries or carriages on the King's Road. Those nightmares would come later.

NIGHTMARES SHOULD
STAY IN DREAMS

ASHTON WAS AWARE of grunting noises and the smell of dusty hay bales and fresh decomposition when he woke. His parched lips thirsted for water, and he quickly remembered where he was and more importantly, where the pig's trough was. He crawled over to it and pushed a large sow over to give him room. He scooped the water into his mouth, trying not to gag at the slick surface and the sticky slobber that coated the lip of the manger shared between the two horses and family of pigs in the barn.

Ashton groaned as he rolled to his side and backed into a hay bale along the wall. He rubbed his fists into his eyes, remembering the strange hallucinations at the burial. The hand from the grave couldn't have been there. Clayton was dead. Ashton had seen the crushed jaw and the gashes across his friend's side and chest. Ashton just hadn't slept. He would walk back to Perketh, apologize to Master Nathan for being late, and pretend he hadn't just freaked out.

Everyone would understand. He was stressed. He hadn't slept the night Clayton had died, and he was obviously exhausted. Master Nathan had probably already started the chainmail order for the local guards. He would of course pick up on that order when he arrived, and Master Nathan could get back to the soft copper bolts and the iron vambraces, which took more skill to produce the delicate curves at the necessary thickness.

A pig grunted from across the barn as Ashton continued to rub his eyes and adjust to the thin beams of light that punctured the barn. As was typical of the area, a craftsman had not been contracted for the job. The farmer and his family and maybe a neighbor or two had pitched in. Nearly every juncture wasn't flush. Light came in from every direction.

Behind him was a window that illuminated the majority of the dirt floor and the center of the room. He realized he must be facing west, since the light from the morning was shining through the window and projecting onto the mess in front of him. The door to the barn was creaking slightly as the breeze moved it back and forth. Birds chirped from outdoors. It was a day like any other, but this time with pigs for company and horses in their stalls, munching on hay and loud, clumsy defecations clopping down the far wall and onto the floor.

Again, a grunt sounded from across the room, but Ashton realized the pigs were near him and around the trough. A sow was now plopped on her side, nursing six piglets. She seemed to be smiling, like pigs often do when they're snorting and nursing. His eyes adjusted to the blinding light from the window behind him, and a darker outline appeared on the far side. A man was there, sitting on a stool.

"Oh geez!" Ashton exclaimed, panicked. "I'm sorry, sir. I'm having a rough couple of days. I ran all night… You see, my friend died. He was my best friend, and I was at his funeral and I—I guess I saw something or thought I saw something. I'll be leaving now. Sorry for the—"

The man grunted again and lurched to his feet. He shuffled forward.

"I didn't touch nothing," Ashton said, standing up and brushing hay from his brown pants with his hands. "I drank some water from the trough, but the pigs didn't seem to mind. I work at a smithy in Perketh. If you need me to pay room and board for the night, I have a coin or two in my pocket."

The man shook his head as he entered the light. Brown, matted hair. He was favoring his jaw with his hand. Ashton knew these facial features. He knew this man. He just couldn't believe what he was seeing. Dirt covered most of the man's body. The left side of his jaw was caved in, and there was a smell about him that wasn't good.

"You're…" Ashton said, stumbling over words. "You're not… You're supposed to be dead."

The creature closed the distance between them, and Ashton shuffled toward the open, creaking barn door. The corpse stumbled forward, tripping over its own legs and hitting the ground hard. It barfed up a vile, putrid liquid that smelled like sheep gizzards. As it coughed and cried out in pain, Ashton bolted for the barn door.

He could hear it spitting back in the barn. It yelled out, and a chill traveled down Ashton's spine, despite his adrenaline and sweat. He cleared the door and slammed it behind him before heading east and then north. He briefly glimpsed along the outside of the barn for a pitchfork, scythe or weapon of some sort, but all he saw was green grass and a fence where a horse whinnied and darted around the enclosure, obviously at least as upset as Ashton was.

Ashton ran north without looking back. He had to put as much distance between him and that thing as possible. Even if that thing was actually his friend, what had happened was an abomination out of his village's worst fables. Common folk were pretty tolerant in Perketh and in the neighboring areas. There hadn't been a witch burning in a hundred years. But a woman with higher farm yield for three straight years was different than raising the dead. There wouldn't be a trial. There would be an execution and a burning at the stake. Maybe both at the same time.

It didn't matter who Ashton was—that he served the community in a respectable profession. There were laws that declared such punishments had to be done. According to people who told stories every weekend in the town square, the only thing more dangerous to the public than a paladin was a necromancer.

But he couldn't be a necromancer! He hadn't brought Clayton back from the dead. It must have been someone else. Someone nefarious. Lurking in the shadows. Casting a spell from afar. That's how they did it in the fables. They weren't crying over a friend's grave. They weren't hovering over morning glories and blue stones!

He couldn't stop thinking about punitive fire consuming his feet, working its way upward. He was a smith's apprentice. He knew the pain of flames. His hands had become accustomed to heat, but they still blistered and peeled when he was clumsy. In truth, falling into a vat of lead or molten pig iron or a forge was one of his greatest fears. He couldn't burn to death. He wouldn't wish that on his worst enemy, and he definitely wouldn't wish that fate on himself.

So, he ran. He ran northeast for the whole morning, stopping only for a mouthful of water out of a stagnant, foul-smelling pond in someone's yard. A crack of a stick somewhere set him off though, and he didn't drink his fill. He stumbled in the mud along the shore, panting hard and swiveling in every direction as he tried to figure out if Clayton had passed him and circled around.

He ran so hard and for so long that he soon found himself in Caller's Forest, some 15 miles east of Perketh. If he kept going this way, he'd eventually reach the elven lands, but he couldn't take another step. He hadn't eaten all day and most of the day before. But his loud stomach growls weren't enough to distract him from the task at hand. As soon as he saw a bed of moss and grass by the side of the road, he fell down into it.

These dreams weren't like the night before. This time, he dreamt of fire and corpses reaching up from the earth. His friend Clayton cursed him for damning his soul to the eternal pits. Dark, oily hands grabbed him and pulled him down into the molten forges. An inferno licked at his legs as the hands tore at his clothes. He fell for ages into the dark abyss, landing hard on his chest and face. When he looked up, a dark figure approached. It hissed at him like a crowd might when a cheater got exposed at cards.

"You took him from me!" the figure accused.

Her makeup was permanent now. Her eye sockets as black as her lips. She was not beautiful like the day before. She was wraithlike and the edges of her ethereal black dress danced like tongues of flame, threatening him as she advanced. A bony finger extended toward him.

"Twice!" she said. "Not just once but twice!"

"I didn't—" he begged her. "I couldn't have!"

"But you did," she accused again.

He couldn't escape. There was nowhere to go. She embraced him with her icy cold arms, and the bottom of her dress enveloped him in dark flames. He screamed as he felt himself pulled into her like a ship into a whirlpool. She did not let go. And deep down, in the core of his being, he knew he deserved it.

A TALE OF THREE ARROWS

ASHTON FELT AND saw light through his eye-lids, but he didn't want to get up. Sure, he hadn't eaten anything in two days, and of course, he had no reason to want to return to his nightmares of Riley pulling him into the underworld. But after being on his feet and running for his life since his best friend's funeral, he didn't think it was too much to ask for just an hour more of slumber.

The bird song assaulted his plans, laying aside any hope of returning to dream worlds. Then there was the cold metal against his neck.

As it dawned on him that he didn't wear a necklace, his eyes flitted open and he unconsciously moved forward, against the metal.

"Careful!" a man warned him.

Ashton found himself staring up a shoddily crafted, soft-edged iron blade. Three figures emerged from the brightness as he adjusted to the morning light.

"What are you—?"

"We're relieving you of your belongings," the man said. "Whatcha got?"

Ashton raised his hand to his eyebrows to shade his eyes so he could get a better look at his brown-haired assailants. The leader, the one who had drawn on him, wore a simple brown tunic with a white but dirty undershirt. One of his henchmen was shirtless and flexing his chest muscles as he thumped a wooden cudgel against his hand. The other man wore a shredded green shirt and loose pants. He held an arrow in a bow aimed directly at Ashton's face. Their faces looked gaunt. They might not have eaten in the past two days either.

"What have I got?" Ashton asked in irritation and gesturing around the empty moss bed he had been sleeping in. "What does it look like I have?"

"No one wanders into the forest with nothing on them," the archer said. "We know you've hidden something 'round here."

"I've hidden nothing," Ashton insisted. "I've been running non-stop for two days!"

"Where you off to?" the bandit leader asked.

"I don't much care," Ashton admitted.

"You get into trouble in one o' the villages, boy?"

Ashton grew silent. He didn't know how to answer that.

The bandit leader laughed and motioned to his friend the archer. "You think this one had something to do with the grave-robbing?"

"Grave-robbing?" Ashton asked.

"Yeah," the burly man with the cudgel said. "He looks like the kind of shit weasel that would claw his way to the underworld…"

"I didn't dig into no grave!" Ashton said.

"Oh yeah?" the archer asked, stretching the bow back farther.

"I'm running from the ghoul that came out of it!"

The bandit leader dropped his sword edge to the ground and took a step back. He smiled and gestured to his comrades. "You hear that guys? Boy's running from a ghoul!"

"I knew those bumpkins from Perketh were crazy," the archer said. "They been telling everyone who comes through town center that a necromancer's on the loose. Say they're going to do something about it!"

The bandit leader and the man with the cudgel laughed and shook their heads.

"Well," the bandit leader said, returning his sword to Ashton's neck. "I guess you could say they've done something with their little witch-hunt. They've sent another dumb kid to us to be relieved of his copper."

"Third one in two days…" the man with the cudgel said.

"Lucky number three!" the archer said, laughing.

Ashton hoped the man was strong enough to laugh and hold that bow so taut at the same time.

"Look," Ashton said. "I don't have any money. I haven't eaten in two days. I'm tired and—"

"We're all tired," the bandit leader said, forcing the dull point of the blade back against Ashton's throat.

"We're all hungry!" the man with the cudgel said, pointing his wooden instrument at Ashton. "And that's where you come in, doesn't it?"

"What you got in your pockets is ours!" the archer agreed.

Ashton rummaged in his torn pockets and unturned each one to show the bandits that nothing was hidden.

"I swear!" Ashton said. "I just want to go home. I've had a really rough couple of days!"

"Oh, life is so hard in the village!" the man with the cudgel mocked in a sweet, high voice.

"I can go inside whenever it rains," the archer mimicked him, finally lowering his bow to join in the jibes.

"What do you do, boy?" the bandit leader asked.

"What do I do?"

"In the village?" the leader added, pointing back to the southwest.

"I'm an apprentice."

"An apprentice to what?"

"A smithy…"

"Master Nathan?" the leader asked, his eyes growing wide.

The two companions whistled loudly and with exaggeration.

"We know your master quite well," the archer said. "Quite a wealthy man, that one."

"Best smith this side of the capital, they say," the bandit leader agreed.

"Can make almost anything," the archer agreed.

"New armor," the man with the cudgel said, pointing at his chest.

"New arrows," the archer said.

"New sword," the leader added. "But you'll find this one, even though it's dull, can still get the job done…"

He slapped Ashton with the flat side of the blade and then returned the point to his neck.

"I'm not helping you," Ashton said defiantly.

"You're not helping *us*?" the man with the cudgel said,

unconvinced. He slammed his weapon inches away from Ashton's hip, startling him.

"You're right," the bandit leader said. He pushed his blade hard against Ashton's shoulder, driving Ashton's back into the moss bed. Ashton grimaced in pain.

"You're helping yourself…" the bandit leader finished.

A rustling in nearby bushes startled the three men, and the sound of heavy footsteps thundered toward them. The archer let loose an arrow, and the attacker took it to the chest, but he kept coming forward. Over his head, the man held a medium-sized boulder, easily as large as Ashton's torso.

"Clayton?!" Ashton yelled.

A second arrow found its mark, but Clayton surged forward, and the bandit leader tripped over a root that crossed the forest path. He held up his non-sword arm to lamely fend off the blow, but Clayton brought the rock down so hard that the man's hand went through his own skull with the rock.

The man with the cudgel swung hard, connecting true against Clayton's shoulder. The foul-smelling ghoul stumbled briefly but recovered with lightning speed. He picked up the boulder from its place atop the bandit leader and hurled it with immense force, striking the strong man in the chest.

The man lost his grip on his cudgel and gurgled blood as he dropped to a knee against a tree stump. The archer let loose a third arrow, piercing Clayton's back, but Clayton continued to walk toward the wounded man.

"Gods, have mercy!" the archer begged, but the Gods had no intentions of answering his call.

Clayton bashed the collapsed man's head in with his own hands until there was nothing left but gobs of hair and brain matter clinging to the tree stump behind his body. By the time Clayton turned around, the archer was gone.

Clayton wheezed and panted as he looked around the clearing.

"Are you ok?" Ashton asked lamely.

Clayton's eyebrows lifted in surprise. He pointed to the arrows and gave a series of muffled grunts and whines. His caved-in jaw wasn't helping with communication, but somehow, Ashton knew exactly what he was saying. Perhaps because after knowing Clayton for fifteen years and hanging out with him every day since, Ashton didn't need anything more than body language.

"It's really you, ain't it?" Ashton asked.

Clayton nodded.

"You're not some spirit?"

Clayton's shoulders sank, and a muffled cry hissed and gurgled out of his mouth or throat.

"I'm sorry," Ashton said.

Clayton dropped to the ground and sat against a large maple tree. His breathing was labored, but he nodded in appreciation.

"No, really," Ashton said. "I'm sorry I ran from you."

Clayton raised two fingers.

"Both times," he agreed. "I'm sorry. Neither of them was called for. I was just scared."

Clayton nodded, shrugging off the slight as only two best friends could do. Ashton knew the issue was settled between them because apologizing and moving on was just something they had always been able to do.

When Clayton earned the head apprentice job over Ashton, it was water under the bridge within minutes. Before long, Ashton was johnny-on-the-spot with Clayton's ingots and kindling. He became Clayton's number one fan in yet another aspect of their lives. When Clayton asked the prettiest girl in the village out, all it took was a simple nod between them, and any protest or claim Ashton might have felt was done. Ashton was happy for Clayton and Riley. He loved them both now, and Clayton most of all.

"How are we going to tell Riley?" Ashton asked.

Clayton sighed through his throat.

"We're going to have to give you a bath or something," Ashton said.

Clayton slightly shook his head, and Ashton laughed in understanding.

"Just because you're dead," Ashton said, "doesn't mean you have to smell like it."

Clayton picked up a small pebble and threw it at him.

"Leave it to me," Ashton said. "We'll figure something out."

All traces of fear were gone as he walked over to Clayton. He grabbed one of the two feathered arrow shafts protruding from his friend's chest.

"Can you feel it?" Ashton asked. "Does it hurt?"

Clayton shrugged. He put a hand against his own shoulder and pushed hard.

"Just pressure? Is that what it feels like?"

Clayton twisted his hand back and forth to signal *more or less*.

"I'm going to pull this out, ok?"

Clayton nodded and braced his arms around the maple tree trunk behind him. Ashton put weight on his heels as he straddled his foul friend and pulled with all his might. The arrow slid bloodily out, and the stench was overwhelming.

"Oh, sweet baby gods!" Ashton exclaimed after breathing in too many of the fumes from the fresh wound. "Bless the altar of the Creator!"

Clayton punched Ashton hard in the shoulder, and he couldn't help but laugh.

Ashton pulled off his shirt and wrapped it around his nose and face. It was coated in dried sweat, dirt and moss pollen, but it was a hundred times better than smelling whatever was coming out of his friend's body.

He grabbed the second arrow in Clayton's chest and repeated the process of gory retrieval. A small trickle of red, black and oozing white came out of the hole.

Ashton dry heaved once, closed his eyes and walked over to a nearby patch of bright orange, black-eyed susans. He snapped them from their stems and returned to Clayton.

"I have to plug the holes," Ashton said.

"Kmmm eeeooon," Clayton protested.

"Don't *come on* me," Ashton replied. "You're leaking all over the place. And you smell. The flowers will help mask the odor."

Clayton continued to protest. Spittle drained down his neck.

"Think about Riley," Ashton said. He pointed toward the lines of blood and pus draining down Clayton's abs. "Imagine how she'd react if she saw and smelled this."

Clayton went silent. He closed his eyes and tears began to form at the corners.

"It's going to be ok," Ashton said. "She's going to be excited to see you—"

Clayton grunted.

"How do I know? Well, I was at the funeral. Could you see us there?"

Clayton shook his head.

"Well, she was the most beautiful thing in the field," Ashton said.

Clayton pushed him on his shoulder.

"You know she's the prettiest creature in the village. She wore a black dress. White makeup. Black eyeliner and lips. I think she wanted to join you in the ground. She was dressed for the part."

Clayton moaned and slurred a response.

"Then she attacked me last night in my dreams."

Clayton raised an eyebrow.

"It was a dream, of course," Ashton said as he turned Clayton to the side so he could grab hold of the third arrow that was lodged in his back. "Very dark. She dragged me to the underworld. I didn't know it was her at first, but she grabbed me. She had all these dark hands, and she scolded me for taking you away from her. And just like you, she held up two fingers and claimed I did it twice. She was angry. She said I had taken you away from her twice!"

Clayton laughed and mumbled something.

"Yeah, it does sound like her," Ashton agreed.

He pulled with all of his might and the arrow came out easily. He patched his friend up with more black-eyed susans, and chiseled into the maple tree with the bandit leader's rusty sword until a steady drip of maple sap coated the blade. He transferred the sticky, sweet-smelling goo from the blade to Clayton's many cuts and openings.

"This will have to do for now," Ashton said, admiring his

work and appreciating the muted smell of death through the shirt that was still wrapped around his head. "Did you see a creek on your way here?"

Clayton nodded affirmatively.

"We'll make our way back there once we find some soap," Ashton said. "I'm betting the bandits had a camp nearby. We'll rummage around there for some supplies. Can you move?"

Clayton got to his feet with some small effort and nodded again.

"Would you mind looking around for an encampment?"

Clayton nodded.

"If you find some food, maybe bring some back. I'm starving. Are you hungry?"

Clayton shook his head and mumbled something incoherent.

"You don't feel pain, and you don't get hungry anymore?"

Clayton sighed.

"Well, that's a good thing right? One less thing to worry about, I guess."

Clayton's mannerisms basically said *yeah, I guess.*

"It'll probably take us a day or so to get back to Perketh if we're walking," Ashton said. "Best to bring something to eat that carries well. Bread. Cheese. Fruit. Might be something in the forest along the way too. Mushrooms, maybe."

Clayton nodded as he lurched down the road. Ashton watched him until he disappeared into some bushes.

"I'm not sure I'm ever going to get used to this," Ashton said as he bent over the mangled bandit leader and finding a copper coin and a wad of chewing weed.

He stepped over the bow that the archer had discarded and held onto the crude, dull iron sword instead. He had never used a bow before. He felt at least somewhat competent with a sword. He and Clayton had sparred with similar training weapons that Master Nathan had made at the smithy.

The man with the cudgel added another farthing. Combined with the copper, he might be able to afford a bar of soap at a general store. Clayton returned half an hour later with a nice leather satchel that the bandits must have lifted from a wealthy traveler. It still had blood spots on it. Inside, Clayton had placed three apples, half a loaf of bread and a chunk of dried beef hide, a crude type of jerky that had been laid out on a rock in the sun.

It was the first meal that Ashton had had in days, and he devoured the jerky and bread so quickly that he fell into a food coma as soon as his body hit the moss bed. As he began to doze off, Clayton pulled the two bandit bodies away from the clearing. Ashton smiled as his eyelids closed. His friend thought of everything.

He woke twice, despite his exhaustion. The first happened during the waning daylight, and the second occurred in the middle of the night. Each time, there was a crunching and tearing sound from the deep woods. He called out for Clayton, and then the noises stopped. Within moments, his friend appeared from the forest, wiping his face and hands on the dark clothing he had stolen from the dead bandits.

"Keep it down," Ashton said absently after the second time. "I'm trying to sleep."

Clayton nodded and made motions for Ashton to settle back down. Ashton rolled onto his side with his back to his friend. He heard Clayton rustle through the branches and trees. Ashton didn't hear any more noises that night—at least, nothing loud enough to wake him.

He dreamt of Riley again, but this time, he didn't panic as she dragged him into the underworld. She started to scream at him, but the look on his face stopped her. The nightmare had changed. The darkness began to dissipate on the walls near him, and a white morning glory poked through. He plucked it from the wall. As he did so, the blackness cleared three feet around it, exposing a vine and two more morning glories. He gathered these as well, and the wall became clearer. Soon, the darkness on the wall had disappeared, and each petal was clearly visible.

Around Riley, there was still darkness, but she shone like a beacon through it. He brought the three flowers to her.

"I'm bringing Clayton back to you," he said. "I'm sorry I took him. Not once but twice."

She smiled with black lips. He noticed her arms and legs were now as dark gray as her dress. Only her painted white face was white as he approached, but when she plucked the morning glories from his fingers, her hands returned to the pale white that he remembered.

He kissed her on the cheek and then sat down beside the back wall, looking at her. She disappeared, and he felt a coldness from her departure. In his own dream, he felt alone. He leaned against the vines and instantly woke up, like cold water had been thrown onto his face.

Clayton sat beside him, staring at him. Clayton must have found a stream, because his dark brown clothes were washed, and he smelled decent. He had also taken one of the bandit's white shirts and wrapped it around his head so that only his eyes showed. Ashton figured Clayton was trying to hide the damage to his jaw.

Ashton stretched and creaked his neck. He checked the

satchel and grinned to Clayton as he saw it had been filled with a change of clothes and still contained the two apples. Ashton changed into the white shirt and the long dark brown cape and pants that must have been from the bandit camp.

"The headscarf is a good idea," Ashton said, pointing toward Clayton's wrapped head. "A bit unusual, though. We'll just have to tell people we meet that you're from Visanth, across the Small Sea."

Clayton nodded.

"You ready to go?" Ashton asked. He surveyed the sun and figured it must be around eight in the morning.

Clayton nodded again. He looked longingly to the west, toward Perketh.

"I know, buddy," Ashton said. "I know."

Two Parts from the Whole

WITH SOME FOOD in Ashton's belly, he moved quickly. Clayton had no problem keeping up, despite his limp. By midday, they passed through the small gate of the town of Corinth. Ashton knew the local blacksmith Harold here because he frequently came to Corinth in search of supplies for Master Nathan. He stopped by out of courtesy, but he didn't stay long as Clayton seemed nervous and anxious to move on. Harold's assistant Arn provided them with a flagon of water for their ten mile journey back to Perketh. Ashton was appreciative, but Clayton didn't seem to need water either.

Ashton explained that Clayton was from Visanth, across the sea, but neither Arn nor Harold seemed particularly interested in anything other than shaking hands. They were busy. No one mentioned a smell, so Clayton must have done a decent job of scrubbing and reapplying flowers to his wounds when he washed up the night before.

As they exited the main west gate, Clayton began to jog. Ashton came along with him. He could sense Clayton's growing excitement. His friend would turn to him, his eyes squinting from the smile hidden underneath the head scarf. The distance went by quickly. Before long, the rolling hills became even more familiar. An oak began to elicit memories of climbing with Clayton when they were children. Certain stone walls nearby still held "secret" treasures of hidden toys and common gemstones they had found digging in the earth.

Then, it was there. Perketh. Shale roofs to the north, where the more affluent lived. Thatch to the south where he and Clayton had grown up. Riley's apartment, their destination, was in the center of town.

Clayton crested the last hill first. It sounded like he was laughing, and then as Ashton caught up, the laughter stopped. Down at the village entrance, on the eastern side of Perketh, a dark-skinned man in a hooded, common tan cape was arguing with a group of five or six local elders. A small pillar of smoke rose from the center of town, and there was a commotion there.

Ashton walked cautiously down the hill. Something felt off. Clayton seemed just as puzzled. As they came closer to the argument, the voice of Mayor Seth Collins and Alderman Jaime Hogsworth carried to them.

"We don't care about your beliefs or customs," Seth said.

"Quite frankly, your kind aren't welcome here!" Jaime agreed.

"This is barbaric!" the dark-skinned man said.

As Ashton drew near, he realized the man was an elf—the first dark-skinned one Ashton had ever seen. He must have been a dark elf from Uxmal, the only known dark elf city, some 200 miles to the northeast, past the wood elven realm in Nomintaur Forest.

"We're in an unprecedented time!" the Mayor said.

"No, we're not!" the elf said. "Not for my people!"

The elf blew aside an annoying strand of white hair that dangled down from his hood.

"What do you know of necromancy?" Jaime asked. "Maybe it was you who did this?"

"Is this true?" Seth asked.

"No!" the elf shouted. "I'm a prince of my people! I have sworn an oath to defy evil magic! I would never!"

"I'll have you know," Seth said, "that we've sent a rider to King Eldenwald."

"If I were you," Jaime said, "I wouldn't be here when the King's men get here."

"I'm telling you," the elf said, "the woman had nothing to do with this. I sensed no magic. None whatsoever!"

"Get out!" Seth shouted.

Someone threw a rock, and the elf reached to his side where a fine white and dulled gold sheath held a remarkable dagger handle. Ashton knew craftsmanship when he saw it. The handle was made out of some white stone or tusk. Intricately carved.

The elf backed away.

"I'm leaving," he said.

"Damned right you are!" someone shouted from behind Seth and Jaime.

The elf moved along the road, away from the small mob, like a viper slithering backward but ready to strike. Ashton placed a hand to his friend's shoulder and guided him along the road with plenty of distance between the elf and Ashton and Clayton.

As the elf caught sight of them in his periphery, he drew his long silvery knife to let them know he was not to be trifled with. A small rock landed some twenty feet away, thrown by one of the townsfolk. The elf snarled, but then suddenly stopped in his tracks as his red pupils fell on Ashton and Clayton.

His dark mouth went agape. Ashton knew that the elf realized something was up. Ashton dropped his own soiled hood back to his shoulders, revealing his face so the people of Perketh could recognize him. He moved quickly toward the Mayor with himself between the elf and Clayton.

"Mayor Seth!" Ashton hailed him. "What's going on here?"

The elf seemed ready to hurl the knife at him, but the closer Ashton got to the village folk, the less sure the elf became. He eventually sheathed the knife.

"You've all made a terrible mistake!" the elf yelled as he turned and ran across a nearby hill, toward the northeast. "Your people will pay for it dearly!"

"Your threats mean nothing!" the Mayor yelled.

"I'm not the one making threats," the elf called as he disappeared down the road.

"Ashton?" a familiar voice asked.

"Master Nathan!"

Ashton clasped his master by the arm and smiled. Nathan was in his usual black leather smock and tan suspenders. He had been working the furnace today, as evidenced by his dark cheeks and suit-covered brown hair. He was not his usual chipper self. He looked worried, maybe even afraid. He seemed to have more lines around his eyes than usual. If Ashton didn't know any better, the water lines down his face looked more like tears from his eyes than sweat from his forehead.

"Who's this?" Nathan asked.

Ashton was so happy to see his master that he had forgotten all about Clayton. Thankfully, Ashton had been working on a cover story for most of the day, even testing it out on people he ran into in Corinth.

"Master Nathan," Ashton said. "This is Crowley of Sevania."

Nathan looked Clayton up and down.

"Burns?" Nathan asked almost mournfully.

Ashton looked at Clayton, who was examining his clothing for scorch marks. Ashton realized his master had thought an accident had befallen his companion. He almost chuckled, but thought better of it. It seemed like a more convincing story, and one that could actually explain Clayton needing to stay under his clothing.

"Yes!" Ashton said, accidentally more enthusiastic than he intended. "He was in training, apparently."

"As a smither?"

"Yes! But he lost his master in a fire. They say he tried to go back into his build three times."

"Brave man!" Mayor Seth said.

"We've lost a master in Sevania?" Nathan asked, worried. "It wasn't Master Aven, was it?"

"No," Ashton said, improvising as quickly as he could. "The master was from Malak in Visanth, across the sea. He came to Sevania in search of work."

"Ah," Nathan said. "I don't know any masters from

Visanth. Still, I'm sorry to hear of your loss, Crowley. Loss seems to be everywhere these days."

Nathan looked at Mayor Collins and then back to Ashton. He tried to smile but his cheeks seemed to fight against it.

"Indeed," Jaime said morosely. "I fear we cannot take anymore here."

Ashton nodded. "I've told Crowley of our loss." He stared at Clayton for a moment longer than he intended. "Of my best friend Clayton."

The Mayor and Alderman cleared their throats.

"Yes," Seth said. "Well—"

Nathan's large, calloused hand flopped against Ashton's shoulder.

"Let's walk together," Nathan said.

He raised his other hand to the Mayor and small group of elders before guiding Ashton into the city. Clayton followed closely behind him. The smells and scents of a barbecue filled his nostrils. It wasn't beef or pork or lamb, though. It smelled sweeter and turned his stomach slightly, possibly because he hadn't had anything of substance to eat since midday, nearly five hours ago.

"We've been looking for you," Nathan said. "We were worried."

"I'm sorry," Ashton said, trying to think of a good excuse for leaving so quickly after Clayton's funeral. "I needed to get out of town. After everything that happened… I… I couldn't see the roads without thinking of him. Everywhere I looked… I… I would see things that reminded—"

"I understand," Nathan said. "No one blames you."

A pillar of smoke from the center of town grew larger over the nearby buildings.

"I may be a bit spotty at work for the next week," Ashton apologized. "Crowley—"

"Take all the time you need," Nathan said.

"Thank you…"

Clayton moaned and grumbled from behind him, but Ashton couldn't discern anything specific without watching his friend's body movements. Nathan still guided him by the shoulder toward the center of the village. Ashton began to feel odd, possibly queasy from anxiety at having to lie to his kind master. Perhaps from worrying about his clumsy explanations, of being found out by the elders of the town.

As they passed the last shale-roofed house on the north side of the street into the main square, a smoldering pile of wood came into view. There were no spits, as you might see in a grill. A single black stake rose from the center. It took a few seconds for the scene to register.

There were chains there and a body.

"What is this?" Ashton asked.

He heard a thud behind him, knees smacking the cobblestones.

A slight breeze blew northward, and black hair billowed in the wind from the stake.

"Master Nathan?"

"Sometime after the funeral," Nathan said, "Someone dug up Clayton. The elders did a door-to-door. Necromancy, as you know, is punishable by death."

Clayton moaned from behind him.

"She hadn't come out of her apartment for two days," Nathan said.

"No," Ashton said. "This can't be happening…"

"She still had the dirt under her fingernails…"

"She had been kneeling beside his grave," Ashton said, tears brimming and draining down his face. "Her hands had probably been in the dirt while the women were bending down to kiss her. She was in mourning… How? Why?"

"There was nothing I could do," Nathan said. "The village was convinced she had dug him up. Taken him somewhere and hid his body. She wouldn't confess to where she had taken him…"

Clayton was openly crying and lashing along the ground.

"Ashton," Nathan said. "What's wrong with your friend?"

Ashton pushed Nathan's hand from his shoulder and grabbed Clayton. His friend refused to stand, and he was too heavy to lift.

"It's the fire," Ashton apologized instinctively. "It affects him…"

"Because of the burns?" Nathan asked. "Gods, I'm so sorry! I just thought you should know…"

Clayton hissed angrily, and Ashton felt his friend growing more rigid and resistive. When he caught Clayton's eyes, he saw red. He saw murder.

"Let me help you carry him," Nathan said.

"No!" Ashton yelled accidentally. "He doesn't like to be touched. He's tender. He'll be ok."

Clayton growled, and Ashton pulled him away from Nathan and toward Clayton's old apartment.

"Take all the time you need!" Nathan called after him. "I'm sorry! I'm so sorry, Ashton!"

The smell was unbearable. Seared flesh. Human. Riley.

Clayton cried openly now and Ashton along with him. "Just another block to the apartment."

Clayton whimpered and sobbed. He stumbled over his feet on the cobblestones.

"We're almost there," Ashton said. "Hold onto me. I've got you."

Ashton pushed against the door, and Clayton tumbled into his old apartment. The place smelled of morning glories and bread. A small stove sat cold in the corner. The last morning glories that Ashton had picked for her on the way to the funeral were on the kitchen table. Riley's wooden lattice along the far wall held dozens of flowers that Clayton and he had brought her over the past three months.

Ashton shook his head, numb with internal pain. This had to be another nightmare. This couldn't be real. He remembered Riley screaming at him from the underworld.

He looked at Clayton, who was now curled into a ball on the creaky wooden planks of the floor. In his dreams, she had accused Ashton of taking Clayton away from her twice. He wondered if she had known that this would happen. He wondered if she had accused him of a crime he had not yet committed. The first when he had asked Clayton to rise from the dirt. The second when Clayton remained in this world while she died in the main square of their home town, at the very hands of the people whom had guided them and loved them all since infancy.

In the last dream, she had looked peaceful after he had given her the flowers from the wall. Her arms and legs had been black, like they were at the stake. Her dress had been black, as her body was now. Her face had been as he had remembered her at the funeral, but her hands had been black until they touched his flowers. She had smiled and then disappeared, leaving him alone in the darkness, like he was now.

He placed his hands on Clayton, rocking him gently back and forth as his friend cried.

"I'm sorry," Ashton said. "I did this."

Clayton moaned from the floor.

"I'm the reason you're back from the grave. I'm the necromancer."

Clayton reached up and hugged him, and Ashton began crying anew.

"It should've been me on that stake," Ashton said. "Not Riley. Me."

They draped arms over each other's shoulders for an hour. A shattered young man and his decaying friend. As the strength in their legs returned to them, they took turns smelling the morning glories on the lattice and then the freshest ones on the table. Ashton packed what few items were still left in the kitchen along with some basic utensils.

"We have to get out of here," Ashton said. "My heart cannot stand another minute."

Clayton nodded and proceeded toward the front door. He opened it, and his shoulders sank. As Ashton caught up, the overwhelming scent of charred death assaulted his nostrils. He grabbed Clayton by the bicep and dragged him through the portal.

"This place is not for us anymore," Ashton said, surveying the buildings as if he had never seen them before, as if they held no special place of love in his soul.

He headed east to avoid the main square, and he kept going past the gate in the picket fences. Clayton shuffled closely behind, his head scarf made from dead bandit's shirts coming looser with each step. The smell of older decay mingled with the fresher charred scent, and Ashton welcomed his friend's undead fragrance over the tragedy of the main square. Anything to mask what happened to Riley. Anything to help him forget what he had caused. The next time she assaulted him in his dreams, he would welcome it. She deserved her retribution, and no collection of morning glories from a wall of darkness would soften what he had done.

He turned to look at the village of Perketh once more as he climbed a nearby hill. Clayton too watched the sunset over the village. When the bright orange dipped below the shale houses, a dark orange turned to red and pink. Like flowers on the horizon.

Ashton sobbed as he returned to the King's Road. Just north was the town of Alefast, famous for its bitter brews. Ashton could think of no better place in the world to be. Perhaps he'd get lucky and drown in one.

WORD REACHES THE KING

KING AETHIS ELDENWALD sat on a red royal pillow in a high-backed marble chair in Kingarth, the capital of the great human kingdom of Surdel. He was bedecked in a black and purple tunic and a white tiger's fur on his shoulders. Around his neck hung a four-point, golden holy talisman supposedly cut from a falling star and given to his family by the monks of Mount Godun, the mountain at the center of his kingdom. His hair was still mostly blond, despite his fifty years, thirty five of which had been spent ruling amidst the politics, wars, and schemes of the four lord governors of his realm.

His gray, wisened advisor Jurgen Drodd sat in the right-hand chair, one step lower. Jurgen was balding and his body weakened by old age. Aethis' wife Shea sat to his left. She was bedecked in a tight-fitting, purple dress with a black cloak wrapped around her shoulders and down the length of the stone chair and the five steps and red carpet at their feet. Below him and along the walls were his Royal Guard in polished silver plating, led by the capable, highly decorated Lord General Godfrey Ross who stood off to the side, looking over his men. Lord Ross's plumed helmet was tucked under his arm. His face was stern, clean-shaven and with a brushed back, ear-length, wavy gray-and-blond hair.

Along the walls behind the King were the princes in their finest armors. In the back corner behind him, a man in dark brown leathers and a simple cape and hat leaned against the wall. His spymaster Theodore Crowe.

An ambassador from the dark elves bowed below the King and Queen.

"King Aethis," the elf said.

"Welcome back to my court, Valedar."

"Your Highness is too kind," Valedar said, his bright green eyes glowing unnaturally in the slight darkness of the chamber. His crimson cloak spread across the floor around him as he kneeled. "I wish I were here under better circumstances."

"You speak of the necromancer?" King Aethis asked rhetorically. "She is of no concern to the dark elves. My people tell me that she is dead, burned at the stake in Perketh."

"Prince Jayden does not believe the matter is resolved," Valedar said. "As you are aware, we take the charge of necromancy quite seriously."

"As do we all," Advisor Jurgen noted in an aged, raspy voice, "but the necromancer is dead."

"Your kingdom forgets," Valedar said. "We dark elves deal with this menace every day."

"We remember our legends," King Aethis said, "and we sit in the shadow of Ul Tyrion. We remember enough and well. There's a more pressing matter in your visit. I find it hard to not take offense that a royal prince of Uxmal would visit my kingdom but not my capital. What was he doing in Perketh?"

"We sensed a person with magical gifts," Valedar said. "Our prince investigated. He found a boy with such gifts but was nearly lynched by your people."

"Are you to tell me," Advisor Jurgen said, "that a dark elf prince was scared of a mob of common humans with sticks and stones?"

"The prince was being diplomatic," Valedar said in his measured, well-educated accent. "We have known peace with humans for over ten thousand years. For two thousand years, our cities have fallen, one-by-one to an alien menace. We fight off a horde while you enjoy the freedoms and tranquility that come with our vigil. From King's Harbor in the west to Edinsboro in the east, from north-most Nortown to southern Sevania, your people number in the hundreds of thousands and in dozens of cities and towns. We have but one city left. Uxmal. In all honesty, Great King, we would not risk the slight to your powerful nation. Our friendship is too direly needed."

King Aethis was taken aback by the envoy's honesty. He looked along the wall at his three sons Magnus, Ragnar and Olaf, all clad in the finest armor he could buy. His wife had also borne him four beautiful daughters: Helen, Janis, Ellen, and Cassandra. They were not present in the throne room. They had their own games and duties to perform. Two were in Visanth. Helen and Janis wooed princes there to keep the peace. Ellen had married Brandon Crayton to reward Lord Bartholomew Crayton for the strength of the bond with the lord of the prosperous northeastern territory. Youngest Cassandra stayed in the library with her books. She refused every suitor her parents sent her way. Aethis doted on her most because of her rebellious spirit and beauty. Shea told him so every day.

The ambassador from the dark elves was right to envy Surdel's prosperity, but the King was not at fault for the dark elves' plight. They claimed to fight demons. According to them, their doom started thousands of years ago with the fall of the one true god and the unleashing of hordes of demons and undead from the underworld. The Creator was gone now. The elves claimed that he no longer answered prayers. He had been banished somehow, long ago.

At least, that's what the dark elves claimed. Aethis knew it only because they insisted he know it for diplomatic relations. He had never seen a demon. He had only heard about them from his spymaster when given reports of whatever random imaginary things the common folks were panicked about this week. Vampires in the mountains. Three headed rodents that breathed fire in the northeast.

"You speak plainly," Aethis said. "So ask me plainly what you want from me."

"Make sure the necromancer is dead," Valedar requested.

Advisor Jurgen guffawed. "The King has already told you she's dead. That should be the end of it."

"You're not magically attuned," Valedar said. "If I were to tell you to test someone for sorcery, you would put them to the fire. If I told you to rid us of a necromancer, you would throw them atop the same flames. We believe you've burned the wrong person. We sense someone else, and if a grave was disturbed in your realm, then we cannot afford to risk a third front opening up to us."

"We have our own issues with the orcs to our southeast," Advisor Jurgen said.

Valedar scoffed similarly to how Jurgen had done earlier. "You are protected by the Southern Mountains. They trickle into your land like ants through a straw. Besides, orcs are not necromancers. Orcs are not sorcerers. They are brutes who showed up alongside the demons beneath us. They raid your villages, and you deal with them with conventional arms. Knights, footmen, and archers. Perhaps you ask the Wood Elves to aid you if you want to lessen your losses. You have allies who come to fight your battles with metal and wood."

"Do you mean to insult me in my chamber?" Aethis asked. "Our friends in the woodland realm honor our call because we are allies. Ask for our aid, and we too would honor your call!"

"I do not mean to offend you or your people," Valedar said, shaking his head. "I mean only to explain why we take this necromancer seriously. We fight only demons, beasts with fiery fangs, claws and eyes. We battle unnatural creatures with control over the undead and terrible magical destruction. Our fight is rarely with sword or lance or mace, unless they are imbued with unnatural properties. Our fight is with magic, and there is no other force we know of in all of Nirendia that we can call to. You have outlawed magic for millennia. What force would you send to help us? The paladins are no more."

"Do not ask me to reform the paladins!" Aethis said. "It is forbidden!"

"Then please," Veledar said, "if you do not wish to offend me just as I do not intend to offend you, do not offer us military aid when you know you have no useful aid to offer,"

The court gasped.

"You mentioned aid, and I am simply trying to convey what we, the remains of the Etyria Empire, need," Valedar clarified, his glowing green eyes darting around the room at the agape mouths of the court. "Our fight with the underworld is ours, for now. What will help the dark elves stand for another thousand years is peace and stability in the world above. Protect our backs while we fight in the underworld. Do not allow this necromancer to take root. Find him. Stop him. Kill him. Do this, and we will hold our lines in the darkness for as long as we can. Do this, and the loss of our sanctuaries from Shamat to Daydira will not have been in vain."

The King rose from his throne and walked to the north window. He gazed up at the ruined fortresses of the dark elven capital of Ul Tyrion. In the legends, its spires were white and hundred foot pennants snapped in the wind, displaying the pink and gray colors of the strong, ancient magical kingdom of Etyria. Now, the crumbling façade was black and almost blended into Ordang Mountain. According to their own histories, Ul Tyrion had been over twice the size and population of Kingarth and capable of magic defenses. Now, it was an uninhabitable ruin.

The dark elves claimed to have detonated the lower chambers of the city, sealing their adversaries in. They had similarly caved the great northern cities of Shamat and Xhonia. Tens of thousands of years of history, gone within a hundred years. A strange blue rock coursed throughout the cities now, barring any entry into its past and secrets. According to the elves, the demons took longer to move east along the northern borders, or perhaps, the dark elven defenses had been stronger there and less prone to surprise attack. But in the histories, Phiol fell five hundred years later. Chejit and Daydira fell some time later, without even a footnote in human history. In truth, the dark elves only appeared before him with bad news. Without constant contact, even close allies could be forgotten.

"Your cities have been gone for a thousand years," Aethis said, "and not once have you tried to reclaim them."

"You go too far," Valedar said, lowering his head and clearly getting emotional. "Each city was fought to the last man, woman and child. A generation of my people were lost trying to reclaim Daydira alone. People who I knew. Great men and women. My master and trainer. Family. Friends. All gone…"

The King turned back to the window and the shadow of the dark elf civilization. He summoned a shadowy figure from the corner of the room. His chief spy and assassin Theodore Crowe walked over and kneeled before him.

"My Lord," Theodore said.

"This quibble over magic with the elves ends now. I want you to go to the southern lands, near the village of Perketh. I want you to look for this necromancer discretely. Find out if he exists. The southern lords Mallory and Vossen are already bitter rivals and taken to petty hostilities too easily. I do not want there to be any misunderstandings about my involvement in their affairs, so you must not be detected."

"I understand, My Lord," Theodore said. He bowed and nodded.

"There," the King said. "Mr. Crowe has been on hundreds of missions. Not once has he failed one of my orders."

"We have heard of Mr. Crowe," Valedar said. "Even amongst the dark elves, his elimination of the Visanth King is the stuff of legend. I'm sure he will find the necromancer, if he still exists, as you say. Thank you."

Theodore nodded ever so slightly toward the elf before disappearing back into the shadows.

Valedar began to rise from his knees, but the King waved him off from the window.

"One last thing," the King said.

"Yes, Great King?" Valedar asked.

"The next time your prince is in my kingdom, I expect him to come to me at once."

Valedar gnawed at his lip and busied himself with re-spreading parts of his cloak. "It is not my place to command our prince."

"Then frame it as a request," Advisor Jurgen suggested.

"That I can do," Valedar said, bowing. "It will be done."

"Perhaps tempt him with meeting my daughters," King Aethis said. "Three are of age and unwed. Hearing of your nation's woes, I cannot help but feel a betrothal may be best for both of our ancient houses. Uxmal cannot stand for long with just Queen Jayla and Prince Jayden in the line of succession. You need royal heirs, and ours is a fine stock."

He pointed to his sons and his beautiful wife. "A breeding stock."

"You are too kind," the elf said, bowing deeply. "Tell me, do any of your daughters perform magic?"

The King's lungs emptied abruptly, as did those of his princes and wife and advisors and courtiers in the room. A murmur spread throughout the room in the corners and shadows, among the nobles. Of course, the elf knew that magic was forbidden.

Advisor Jurgen twirled his white beard and adjusted his pointed purple hat. He cleared his throat awkwardly. "The King's daughters are not proficient in magic."

"What of his sons?" the elf asked without a trace of sarcasm. "Perhaps my Queen may discuss taking another husband. She's been widowed over a thousand years. Her period of mourning is long over. A magical son may bring us prosperity and hope. Our empire is in dire need of another capable wizard who might help us hold back the tide."

Whispers echoed across the stonework in the throne room. A prince wielding magic would have been a scandal.

"No," Aethis replied simply.

Valedar sighed.

"I will tell Queen Jayla and Prince Jayden," Valedar said, "of your request for suitable marriage. I am sure that the next time our prince comes to the land of Surdel, he will make his presence felt at your court. I offer you my humblest apologies for his absence. I will assure Prince Jayden that no mob will be waiting for him when he returns to your lands. Perhaps, when next he visits, he might visit with your princes and princesses."

"We will reaffirm to our lords," Advisor Jurgen said, "that no dark elf will be harmed under penalty of death, unless in lawful provocation. Will that ease your mind and that of your Queen and Prince?"

Valedar bowed deeply toward Jurgen, the King, the Queen and each of his sons.

"We are most grateful for your hospitality," the elf said.

"Feast with us tonight," the King said. "Tomorrow, we will send word to the southern lords that a suspected necromancer is loose and that we expect them to aid in our search for this man. We will post rewards on posters in public gathering places. Theodore will conduct his own investigation."

"Thank you, King," Valedar said before bustling out of the chamber.

The court caller announced that all official business was concluded for the day, and King Aethis motioned for his advisor, spymaster, and his three sons to join him in the antechamber where court business was really done.

The King entered first, followed by his oldest son Magnus, already a twenty-three-year-old man, then teenage Ragnar, and the youngest boy Olaf. Advisor Jurgen hobbled into the room as he supported his seventy-year-old frame, and Theodore Crowe closed the door after Queen Shea and King Aethis kissed each other's hands and waved goodbye.

"So," the King said to his advisory panel. "What do you really think?"

His valiant son Magnus, already a well-regarded war hero from his exploits along the orcish border at the most recent battles of Dragonpaw and Hell's Gate, spoke first. "He seemed honest."

"Bah!" Jurgen said. "You're just a boy!"

Magnus's broad shoulders sported the same size adult male tiger head and coat as his father. He appeared non-plussed by Jurgen's insult. Aethis grabbed his son by the shoulder and smiled, letting him know that he felt the same.

"The southern lords are growing restless," Theodore said. "Our spies in Mallory Keep tell me that Mallory has been funding bandit parties all along the forests between Alefast and Perketh in the west. They are explicitly tasked with raiding Vossen's tax payments."

"That makes it the King's business, doesn't it?" Magnus asked. "Should I lead a party of knights down to clear them out?"

"Why is Mallory preventing my tax payments?" the King asked. "My son is right. I cannot let this stand."

"I can assure you the tax payments are being made," Advisor Jurgen said.

"Indeed," Theodore said. "Vossen has begun sending two separate tax shipments to Kingarth: one along a westerly route through King's Harbor and Deacon and the other through Alefast and Foxbro. The Foxbro dispatches are being intercepted one out of every two times, off the King's Road. The payments through Deacon are taking weeks of additional travel time but are more reliable. I'm surprised he's not just shipping them across the lake. As far as I know, there are no pirates there to be paid by Mallory. At least, not yet."

"Vossen must have the patience of a saint," Jurgen noted.

"He's a better man than most," Theodore said. "However, he's at his limit. I have a man in the lower court at Vossen Hold. Vossen's youngest son Elliot was captured in one of the latest raids near the King's Road. The ransom was apparently quite high. Vossen knows Mallory is behind it. He's almost ready to send troops."

"And the ransom was paid to Mallory?" King Aethis asked.

Theodore nodded.

"If the raids were along the King's Road," Prince Ragnar said, "then that's royal property. We are not obligated to respond?"

"No," Theodore said. "Technically, the raids took place while the caravans were resting off the road. Each of the raids has happened on Vossen's land. Whenever he sends a mounted force, the forests are empty."

"Quite vexing," Jurgen said.

"Terribly," Theodore agreed. "By the laws of the land, we are not allowed to interfere in business between lords on their own lands. Of course, my King may decide to intercede if he likes."

"Do we know the source of this animosity?" Aethis asked. "These men have been longtime allies. Both came to the aid of Lord Croft at Dragonpaw and Hell's Edge, along with my sons Magnus and Ragnar."

"The Vossen family is not entirely close to the Mallories," Jurgen said. "They have refused to marry their sons and daughters with the Mallories for centuries."

"Why?" Aethis asked.

"Who knows?" Jurgen asked rhetorically.

"150 years ago," Theodore said, "Lord Jaxar Mallory had a young lord killed in the Vossen clan for insulting his daughter. She was apparently very plain, and this young man was the object of her affection and very disinterested. The Vossens had a revenge killing or two with lower court members sympathetic to the Mallories, but they lost another Vossen son trying to kill the daughter for causing the dispute. The blood feud died, but the hatred continues."

"But they fight together against the orcs?" Aethis asked. "A common enemy unites them."

"The blood feud is dead," Theodore said, "but the Vossen's still use the story as an educational tool in the upbringing of children. They do not intermarry because they are taught to hate the Mallories."

"Seems petty after 150 years," Aethis said.

"Does it?" Jurgen asked. "Giving how the Mallories are forcing the Vossens to make two tax payments?"

"What kicked off this latest feud?" Aethis asked.

"The latest orcish incursion was apparently the source of the dispute," Theodore said. "Mallory claims that Vossen owes him for passage and back pay for food and shelter through his lands. Vossen claims he was responding to the King's call to fight the orcish invasion, and no such levy should be made. He claims the King's coffers should pay for the tolls and levies."

"So, Mallory is collecting the tax from Vossen through banditry?" Aethis asked.

"Not officially," Theodore said, "and to reveal that we know this would reveal my sources. I advise caution in publicly accusing Lord Mallory."

"I'm the King," Aethis said. "If I felt there were wrongs here, I would do more than accuse."

"Of course, My Lord," Theodore said, nodding deferentially.

"How exposed are we to open warfare within our ranks?" Aethis asked.

"Vossen won't move against Mallory until he has proof," Theodore said, "but from what I'm hearing from my spies, that is the only thing stopping retribution. For now, Vossen is willing to bide his time."

"Have Lord Croft or Crayton declared?" Aethis asked.

"My spies in either hold have been silent on Vossen and Mallory," Theodore said. "Crayton discusses only the weather and harvests. He does not appear at all interested in the activities of the southern lords, and they have not attempted any communication with him. Croft worries about orcish attacks and the activities of the wood elves."

"What does he have against the wood elves?" Magnus asked. "They were most helpful to Croft in breaking the siege of Dragonpaw. Their five hundred archers kept the orcs at bay."

"And now, they harass his wooden walls with warning shots," Theodore said.

"Why would they be firing at Croft?"

"A perceived slight," Jurgen said. "Croft and the King's men chopped down about twenty acres of trees from the forests west of Nylelthalas. They needed the timber for walls and arrows."

"And this forest was in the elven lands?" Aethis asked.

"Disputed," Jurgen said, "but never with any force from our side. We've always considered it their land. The problem comes from the fact that the elves did not protest the cutting at the time. Apparently, they assumed we would replant."

"How much will it cost?" Aethis asked.

"5,000 gold pieces if we were to supply maples or some other common tree. Probably six months of labor for one to two hundred peasants. Fifty guards should do, in case orcs make incursions."

"The problem is," Theodore Crowe said, "they don't want maples. The original trees were ancient and the wood elves claim they were magical and communicated with the Creator. They claim each tree will have to be replanted from seeds of a fae tree of Nylelthalas, Felsari, or Yla Aiqua."

"Which are sacred to them," Aethis said, realizing the issue. "They would never allow humans to get too close."

"Correct, My King," Theodore said. "The elves consider the trees that were cut down invaluable. Priceless. They claim it will take them hundreds of years to recultivate. They claim they did not protest because they were in shock."

"What do they want?" Aethis asked.

"An apology," Jurgen said, "and the promise that the forest will never be touched again."

The King grumbled. "Does this have to be in person?"

"That would require you getting close to the fae trees," Jurgen said, smiling, "and you're human. One of your only faults."

"The elves are such bizarre creatures," Magnus complained. "I'll never understand them."

"You only need to understand that they are loyal allies," Aethis said, "until they're not. These kinds of slights can fester and erode an alliance. Being a king is all about the details."

"Some say a poor king," Jurgen said, nodding in agreement, "cannot see the forest for the trees. I say a wise king must see the forest but also appreciate the trees. Literally so, in this case."

Aethis smiled at Jurgen, acknowledging the compliment.

"Have an apology ready for me," he said, "and I'll sign. Make sure it is spread to Croft and the southern lords so such a situation is not repeated."

"Understood," Jurgen said. "Most excellent!"

"And offer them a thousand saplings to be planted as they see fit," Aethis said. "Obviously not in this section of the forest, but we leave it to their discretion. Also, remove our dispute from the land. If they have been taking care of it, then I officially recognize that their claim is valid. That should remove any obscurity with who owns the land."

"How shall I mark the transaction, My Lord?" Jurgen asked, opening a ledger he had kept in the folds of his orange robe.

"Recompense for the siege relief at Dragonpaw," Aethis said. He nodded to his son Magnus so that he might pay attention to the wording and the reasoning. Magnus was next in line to the throne.

"What of the necromancer?" young Olaf asked. He was outgrowing his small tiger fur shoulders. Soon, he might have to trade out for the large male tiger furs that his father and two brothers wore. He was the youngest of Aethis's children, some five years younger than Cassandra.

"Any chance he's a ploy of Vossen or Mallory?" King Aethis asked.

"If so," Theodore said, "then they are playing their cards close to their chest on that one."

"Likelihood of that?" Aethis asked.

"Slim to none," Theodore said.

"Why?" Magnus asked. "If Mallory is willing to openly defy peace by paying bandits to steal from Lord Vossen, would it not be within reason to suspect Mallory might fabricate such a story to further impugn Vossen's character to the King?"

"The necromancer, if he exists, appeared in Perketh, which is in Mallory's lands," Theodore said. "The only person who might be impugned here is Mallory."

"And Vossen is incapable of doing such a thing to Mallory?" Magnus asked.

Theodore seemed to ponder the possibility for a moment, scratching the stubble on his face. "All men have their breaking points. Still, necromancy is too taboo a subject. I expect Vossen's retribution to be very direct. Nothing about his character points to this kind of deviousness. Mallory, perhaps, but not Vossen."

"So," Aethis said, "The necromancer is either the figment of the imagination of some jumpy villagers or a real man that even the dark elves fear to have on their flanks."

Theodore nodded. "Still, even if he is real, we have only one report of a grave disturbed. It's possible this was a grieving widow, as the villagers claimed, who stole her husband's body and was burned for it. Or it could be a vendetta against this man, a smith's apprentice, for some deal gone bad, by claiming he is undead to tarnish his name and get his wife killed. At best, you have lost a loyal subject over a witch hunt, which happens. At worst, you have a single necromancer with a single corpse. This is hardly the stuff of legend. It is likely a low game by meaningless players."

Jurgen nodded in agreement. "The last known necromancers were documented during the fall of Ul Tyrion, which casts its shadow upon Kingarth, over a thousand years ago. The elves say the number of undead summoned there was beyond counting. Legends are always exaggerated, but I see no reason to make a huge fuss about this lone man or woman. There is only risk in acknowledging modern necromancy publicly. No reward. From the report of Mr. Crowe, we need less anxiety in the south, not more."

King Aethis nodded as he paced along the stone steps near a large wooden table with red and gold cloth tapestries of knights on tigers fighting huge orcs with giant axes and swords.

"How much is the supposed debt between Vossen and Mallory?"

"A year ago," Theodore said, "the claim was 1,000 gold. Now? Mallory claims 1,500 to 2,000 in his council chambers."

King Aethis tapped Jurgen on the shoulder. "Pay Mallory 1,000 gold. Make it clear that it is for the transport of troops through his lands for the orcish sieges. This should resolve the issue."

"Quite so," Jurgen agreed. "With you claiming the debt, Mallory will have no recourse but to drop his banditry and accept the debt is no longer Vossen's. Any additional claim above the 1,000 would need to be taken directly to your court, which he will not do for it would imply that he believes you did not value his services correctly."

"I believe it will calm the situation," Theodore agreed. "He will swallow his pride and move on to other things."

"It is settled then," King Aethis said, putting his arm around Magnus and walking alongside him as they left the room. He pulled his son to the wall beside the door and motioned for Magnus to listen for ongoing conversations inside as they exited.

"Are you still going to search for the necromancer?" Jurgen asked Theodore as Ragnar and Olaf followed their father through the doorway, falling in line farther down the wall from their oldest brother and the King.

"He gave me a direct order in front of the nobles," Theodore said. "To appease the dark elves, I must do so, and I must be clumsier than usual so word reaches the necessary people."

Jurgen chuckled as he hobbled after Aethis. "Poor spymaster!"

Aethis nodded to Jurgen and Theodore as his spymaster closed the door and locked it.

"I promise I will let you get back to the shadows as soon as I can," Aethis said.

Theodore grumbled but smiled good-naturedly as he strode quickly across the court and down the hallway to the stairs that led to the main gate. Aethis knew that Theodore was aware of his eavesdropping and the lessons he was imparting to his children. It was part of a game they had played thousands of times over the years.

GAZING UPON OUR LORD

ASHTON WOKE TO a migraine and a hangover. Sunlight reflected off a polished surface beneath him. His first thought was not that he didn't know where he was. The more he wakened, the more he remembered he was still in Alefast. His first thought was relief that he couldn't remember dreaming.

Riley had been haunting him even before he and Clayton had found her in the main square in Perketh. Now, she sometimes invaded his waking thoughts. He had been hiding from her memory ever since. Inebriation seemed to be the only thing working anymore.

The soft thud of wooden mugs being restacked forced Ashton to lift his head.

"You know," the innkeeper Brian of the Laughing Barmaid said, "when you told me you wanted a room for two weeks, I expected you'd be sleeping in your room."

Ashton groaned. He blinked repeatedly as the sun assaulted him through the nearby glass windows.

"Now that the two weeks is up," the innkeeper said, "I feel it's best to give you some advice while you're sober. You're a young man. Whatever you're running from, whatever has happened, life moves on. No one, not even a man as young and strong as you might think you are, can survive long in this world on ale and bad thoughts."

Ashton's shoulders hung low. He nodded as he rubbed his face.

"You could die," the innkeeper added.

"Am I still paid up for the day?" Ashton asked.

Brian nodded.

"So I can have another mug?" Ashton asked.

Brian subtly shook his head, as if in disappointment, and then nodded.

"It's just to make the headache go away," Ashton grumbled. "After that, I'll leave."

"Is your friend still waiting on you outside?" Brian asked.

"You know about Clayton?"

"The whole town knows about Clayton," Brian said. "Once you get past your third ale, you won't shut up about him."

"What've I said about him?"

"Trained with you as a blacksmith in Perketh. Married a beautiful girl. That kind of stuff."

Ashton grunted and pointed toward a mug along the wall behind Brian. The innkeeper nodded and slapped the polished wooden bar, which caused Ashton to wince in pain from the migraine. Brian moved the mug under one of the three casks behind him, unplugged the container, and the sound of liquid hitting wood filled the hall.

Ashton breathed deeply, taking in the slightly sour smells of barley mixed with nearby grasses. The fragrance had been unpleasant when he first arrived in Alefast, but now, it brightened his morning. Definitely an acquired taste.

"So, I guess I've told you about Riley then?"

"Who's Riley?" Brian asked cordially, laying the brimming mug down in front of him. "Is she your girl?"

Ashton shook his head.

"So, I've talked constantly about Clayton…"

"Constantly," Brian agreed.

"But in all the nights I've been here, I haven't mentioned Riley?"

Brian shrugged. "Not by name."

Ashton nursed the mug in his hands and leaned over it until his nose almost touched the liquid. He inhaled and exhaled slowly, so powerfully that the churn in the froth hit his nose. The pressure behind his eyes shifted, and the migraine ebbed.

"She was Clayton's wife," Ashton said.

"Oh?"

"She died," Ashton said before taking his first sip. The beverage was bitter but familiar. He immediately felt better.

"Is that why your friend is sleeping in the streets?" Brian asked. "Is he punishing himself?"

Ashton panicked as he realized that he should have had a cover story for this. He had been so engrossed with his own melancholy at raising his friend from the grave, then also being the source of Clayton's wife's death, that he had focused on the task of forgetting his troubles. He had simply wanted to be anonymous for a while and immerse himself in oblivion. No one should have to explain themselves in oblivion.

"You tell your friend to come in here," Brian said. "You tell him that he can stay tonight for free."

"No, we need to be going anyway. I—"

"What kind of friend lets his friend stay outside in the cold?"

"You don't understand," Ashton said. "He's..."

Ashton stumbled over and explanation. He almost said *undead*. Thankfully, his brain worked just well enough to hold the thought back from his lips. He gulped a third of the mug and kept it between his hands.

"He's what?" Brian asked, gripping the counter and peering at Ashton intently.

"He's mourning," Ashton said simply. "He doesn't want to be around people. He wants to suffer."

"Hasn't he suffered enough?" Brian asked. "Losing his wife?"

"It's a phase," Ashton said. "He'll pull through it."

He drank another third of his ale.

"You're right though," Ashton said. "This has to stop. Him sitting outside... Me being in here drinking..."

He looked down at the remaining liquid as he swirled it around his mug. The pressure in his skull had faded enough that he felt he could rise from his oaken bar stool.

"I don't think I need this anymore," Ashton said.

He put the mug down and stepped away a bit too quickly. He grabbed onto the bar to steady himself, and Brian raised an eyebrow. Ashton backed away.

"Until we meet again," Ashton said.

He exchanged a short acknowledgement nod with the bartender. Ashton turned toward the exit, crossed the hall and pushed the heavy door outward. The day bombarded him with warmth and overwhelming light. He covered his eyes with a dirty hand. He smelled his stained brown gray tunic and realized he needed a major change in scenery and attire.

He found Clayton three streets over, sitting in the shade of a building. Unlike Ashton's alcohol-soaked clothing, Clayton smelled of flowers and soap. He must have bathed in a nearby creek or maybe even King's Lake.

Clayton groaned as he got to his feet.

"It's time to go," Ashton said.

Clayton nodded in agreement. He pulled the tattered cloth tighter across his mouth, seemingly afraid that it might fall down and expose the wounds on his jaw.

"There's only one problem," Ashton said. "We can't go back to Perketh. She..."

He couldn't finish the sentence. He might have said several things, but they all failed to form in his throat. She's dead. She's gone. She might still be in the square.

"Where do we go from here?" Ashton said. "What am I supposed to do now?"

Clayton nodded again. He grabbed Ashton by the hands and looked into his eyes. All Clayton did was nod, but an understanding passed between them.

Don't worry about it, his friend seemed to say. *Just follow me.*

Over the course of the day, Clayton guided him away from the pubs and east toward Axewane, south through Suri and then toward Hell's Edge. Ashton had never been this far from Perketh and nowhere near this close to the base of The Southern Peaks: orc territory—the stuff of nightmares. He was more than relieved when they headed back west and south of Corinth. Relieved but confused.

"I'm as loath to go to Perketh as you are," Ashton said as they entered the woods Southwest of Hell's Edge, "but if you think we have to go there, we have to go there. Why the roundabout route?"

Clayton shook his head vigorously. He nodded and pointed toward a limestone keep poking out of the tops of the trees.

Ashton had never been this far south, but he knew that only one southern lord lived north of the harbor of Sevania and southwest of Hell's Edge. Lord Mallory: the man who killed Clayton with his carriage.

They walked along the winding road from Hell's Edge to Mallory Keep for two days, only stopping to eat and sleep in the woods. The area was plentiful with game and edible plants, and they hadn't run into a bandit party since Clayton killed the men in Caller's Forest. Clayton came back from the darkness with two rabbits every night. Ashton always cooked them over a fire and offered one back to his old friend, but each time, Clayton refused. So, Ashton saved it for breakfast, which is what he expected Clayton had intended.

At first, Ashton thought Clayton wasn't eating, and he thought this was just one of the changes his friend was going through. Clayton could no longer walk well, and he couldn't communicate verbally anymore. He didn't appear to sleep much, if at all, and he was far more sullen than he had ever been when alive.

However, Ashton knew his friend had to be eating something. The most obvious evidence was the pools of blood that Clayton left when he went to the bathroom. There's no way all of that blood came just from Clayton. He didn't have that much blood in him. The other evidence came from the occa-sional screams from the forest, usually at night.

Clayton would wait until Ashton lay down for the night, and then, he'd sneak off somewhere. Ashton thought Clayton was keeping guard, and perhaps he was, but Ashton had a sus-picion that Clayton was hunting for food instead. Something with a lot of blood and that screamed almost like a person when you brought it down. Something big. A deer, maybe. An elk. He hoped Clayton might share such a meal with him sometime. A slab of deer would be a welcome change to his diet of nuts, berries, mushrooms and the occasional squirrel or rabbit.

He found out what Clayton had been eating via second-hand, overheard conversations. They had camped a few hun-dred feet from the edge of the forest with the parapet and cur-tain wall of the castle clearly in view. Far away, Ashton heard the jingling of coins against wood and the creaking of wheels. As he and Clayton approached the cacophony, voices carried into the trees.

Ashton crouched down and watched as the armored car-riage approached. It bore the king's purple colors, and along the driver's box were white furs. The golden royal seal gleamed in the morning sunlight. Ashton thought it highly curious that a king's carriage would be carrying gold to a Lord and not the other way around, since money tended to flow upward. Maybe from Ashton and Clayton to Lord Mallory, and from Lord Mallory to the royal family but not vice versa.

The coach had two men in the front, both dressed finely in purple and brown leathers. One held a bow at the ready while the other carried the reins to the two horses.

"I'm telling you the forest is unusually quiet," the archer said.

"It's just morning," the driver said. "Everything's sleeping. Feel free to join them."

"Not a single bandit the whole way from Alefast to Dona," the archer said, looking at the woods as if the trees themselves might jump him and demand toll. "They tend to make themselves known, even if they would never dare directly rob the King's shipments. They'd ask for a bribe, at least."

"You're complaining about a lack of bandits?" the driver asked.

"It's just unusual," the man replied. "I've taken this route as a teamster many times. That's why the king allocated the five gold pieces for this leg of the journey."

Ashton exchanged a look at Clayton. Clayton avoided his eyes.

"Perhaps Lord Mallory cleared them out," the driver said. "He knows we're coming. He wouldn't want anything endangering the King's payment."

"Maybe," the King's archer said incredulously.

"You don't think Lord Vossen killed them all, do you?"

The man with the bow wrinkled his nose and forehead. "You know… that never occurred to me. Just like Lord Mallory knew this payment was coming, so did Lord Vossen. He'd be even keener on making sure the money made it through, I reckon."

"I've heard they've both raised bandit armies," the driver agreed. "Set 'em on each other, pillaging the roads between small towns. Harassing each other."

"The games of Lords," the archer said, "bunch of idiots!"

The carriage went on. Ashton looked at Clayton, waiting for his friend to acknowledge the contents of the conversation.

"They say bandits frequent these woods," Ashton said, "but we haven't come across any, and neither have they…"

Clayton shrugged. He very briefly looked at Ashton but otherwise kept his eyes on the ground or somewhere else in the woods.

"The pools of blood?" Ashton whispered. "Are you the reason there are no bandits in these woods?"

Clayton's brown eyes met Ashton's, and there was shame there. There was a kind of simmering anger and confusion, but shame too.

"OK," Ashton said. "OK."

Clayton mumbled and whined something unintelligible.

"It's alright," Ashton said, placing a hand on his friend's shoulder. "I'm sure they were bad men…"

Part of him believed that. The other part didn't want to think about the implication. Clayton had obviously never eaten anyone when he was alive. If Clayton was eating bandits, then something fundamental had changed inside of his friend. He wondered what else had changed with Clayton and desperately wished he could have a real conversation with his friend.

Ashton appreciated not being involved in or having to watch those meals. He felt bad enough about the label of necromancer. The last thing he needed was the thought of being a necromancer raising cannibals. He took some comfort instead in realizing that what Clayton was doing was making them both safer. He was getting rid of threats. Fewer arrows pointed at them. Fewer swords at his throat when he woke in the morning, as happened in Caller's Forest. There was a noble purpose somewhere in this act. Somewhere.

The carriage rolled down the road toward the main gate, which opened about a thousand feet from the edge of the trees. Between them and the rolling fortune on wheels was a beautiful, rolling green hill with gold, purple and blue flowers dotting the surface of the meadow. The white and orangish-brown brick of the castle walls looked clean and pristine. Guards leaned against the parapet, hailing the driver and archer as they passed underneath.

Ashton and Clayton sat down in the sun, looking at the castle.

Ashton felt a pain building in his chest, a feeling that fought against the warmth of the sun, the smell of spring, and the jokes and commotion of the people above and behind those walls.

"This seems so unfair," Ashton said. He picked at the grass beside him as he continued to look at the castle.

Clayton grunted.

"Behind those beautiful walls, protected by all these men, is the man who killed you," Ashton said. "He's inside there, eating a nice fat steak. His wife is probably laughing with her friends. His children are probably riding horses in these woods somewhere."

Clayton gave a softer grunt—more of an acknowledgment.

"For taking your life," Ashton said, "Lord Mallory will never receive a punishment. He might have been late for a stroll in his gardens. He might have had no particular reason to be in a hurry. According to the law, you were just unlawfully in his way."

Clayton was silent. He put his palms against the grass behind him, propping himself up.

"But giving you back your life," Ashton said, "Somehow, that's deemed worse than taking it. Lord Mallory took you away, and then when I somehow got you back, they took Riley away. An innocent woman. This doesn't seem fair... Is this all we can look forward to in our lives?"

Clayton grunted. He pointed toward the castle and back to himself. From a sort of unspoken language between them, Ashton knew what Clayton had said. *I'm thinking the same thing. That's why I brought us here.*

Ashton nodded.

"I don't think they're done taking from us," he said. "When they realize you really did rise from your grave... When they find out that Riley wasn't the one who brought you back..."

He let the statement hang there.

Clayton shook his head. Again, Ashton knew what he was thinking. *I won't allow it.*

Ashton picked a blade of grass from the earth and threw it over his shoulder. "We're just two guys. We're not even fully trained blacksmiths. We have no money. We have no power. We're nobodies."

Clayton looked down and then up at Ashton and nodded. *You do have power.* He pointed at himself.

"You're not supposed to be here," Ashton said somberly. "I can't ask you to be a part of this. Riley is waiting for you. Maybe it's time we put you back into the ground..."

Clayton looked at Ashton briefly and then returned his gaze to the high walls and the gate that was closing behind the carriage. He slowly shook his head.

"Nrrrooo," Clayton said with some effort. "No."

Ashton nodded in understanding. Clayton felt he had something left to do. Perhaps, some type of justice for Riley or maybe for his own death in the streets of Perketh. Maybe the loss of the beautiful children that might have come from him and his dark-haired wife.

"Someone should be held accountable," Ashton said. "If not for the accident with the carriage, then at least what the people of Perketh did to Riley."

Clayton closed his eyes and moaned softly. Ashton reached across Clayton's back and pulled him closer, ignoring the pungent smell of decay that lingered under the mingled perfume of daisies, dandelions, and black-eyed susans. Clayton cried on Ashton's shoulder, and Ashton patted and squeezed his friend's shoulder. They stayed there in the grass for the better part of the afternoon, watching the sun rise and hang high overhead before beginning its descent.

"Let's get out of here," Ashton said finally as he stood up. "I'm getting hungry."

Clayton nodded as he too got to his feet.

"We may have to go east a bit to find you a good bandit though," Ashton joked.

Clayton playfully punched Ashton in the arm, and Ashton smiled in return as they walked side-by-side on the road north toward Dona and Perketh.

THE LORDS MALLORY

J ULIAN SAT UP in his soft, silken bed on the top floor
of Mallory Keep. He could still hear the phantom creaking wheels jostling along cobblestones from his nightmare. His long black hair clung to the sweat dripping down
his chest, shoulders and back. He rubbed his palms against
his eye sockets and face before pulling aside his stylish white
and black sheets and slipping into a pair of dark sandals. His
loose white blouse and pajama bottoms rustled quietly against
his skin.

He hadn't been able to sleep well since he had poked
his head out of the carriage and seen the young man being
dragged behind it in Perketh. He always woke to the faint
smell of flowers and the sound of pained cries drowned out by
the horse hooves.

He had no fear of punishment, at least not by any court.
He knew a lord always had the right of way on the roads. His
father had told him as much. His tutor Kratos had reiterated

the same, but both of their looks had been hard. They were disappointed. Ultimately, it was his father's judgement that kept Julian up at night.

"Death happens," his father had said coldly upon hearing of the accident. "Laws are for the common folk. Murder is often necessary. But when you kill, son, make it count for something. Did this death count for something? Did it further your goals? Did it move our family closer to something?"

Julian had no idea how to answer his father at the time, so he had said nothing. The death was an accident, but Julian knew he was at fault. He had asked the driver to speed up as they passed through Perketh. Not because he had anywhere to be in a hurry. He just wanted the noise.

He opened the door to the main corridor that connected the three remaining members of his family. He listened at his father's door across the hall for any kind of movement inside, but it was late—maybe two or three a.m. No guards patrolled this floor. They remained on the terrace and stairs unless called upon, and he had no need of them at this hour.

He walked softly down the hall, past the empty rooms of his dead brothers, casualties of the aggressions of the orcs. Past his mother's unused room—the same one that his father's previous wife had inherited before her own untimely death. He knew what the servants claimed. He felt the truth revealed every time his father looked at him coldly, matter-of-factly. A silent reinforcement of what Julian thought about himself and his family. Whatever a man in the Mallory family wanted, he got, no matter the cost. Still, the human part of him felt guilt when there was collateral damage like this. This time, again, he got what he wanted, and someone else paid a price. Soon, he felt it would be his turn to feel the pain of his decisions.

He stopped in front of the wooden door with the dark brown stain that ran down it like dried blood at the end of the hallway. It was his half-sister Jayna's room. She was the only other person in the carriage with him that day. She alone would understand why these nightmares continued.

He tested the knob, and the door creaked inward. A sliver of light broke into the chamber, illuminating Jayna's sleeping form in the high feather bed. White drapes hung from the four poster bed and framed the crimson sheets that matched her fiery hair and spirit. The darkness retreated across her face, and her eyes opened. He smiled and she returned it warmly as he closed the door, immersing the room in darkness.

"Nightmares again?" she asked without a hint of drowsiness.

She had been awake.

He nodded as she propped herself against her pillows, her sheets pressed firmly against her chest. The glow of soft moonlight hit her shoulders from a nearby window. She noticed him looking.

"It'll go away," he lied. "I'll forget."

"If only you'd let yourself," she said. "You have the power to stop them."

"You know I can't do that," he said. "How many times have I tried?"

She grinned and let the covers fall, exposing her naked breasts.

The last time he had seen her nude had been in the carriage that day. He had asked the driver to speed up as she had taken off her dress. The vibrations of the carriage always put her in a mood, ever since they had been fifteen and sixteen. He had only wanted the rattling carriage to mask the sounds from inside, to keep the driver from reporting what they had hidden from their father for nearly a decade.

"Why can't I resist you?" he asked sullenly.

"Why do you feel you must?" she asked. "Do you really think father would disapprove?"

"Yes," he said.

"Why?"

"Because he wants to marry you to some other lord to gain favor and prestige," he said. "He still has hopes of securing an heir to a major house."

"I don't want some other lord," she said, "and besides, a dowry costs money from his estate. Money he can't hand to you when he's gone."

"Fine," he said, "because you're my sister. Because we're both of his blood."

"Is there any other blood that I should be?" she asked, turning toward him as she slipped from her silken sheets. "Is there any other man I should want?"

Julian gulped hard.

"We're doing nothing wrong," she said as she left the bed and walked slowly toward him. He felt her own longing, an irresistible pull between them. "Only love."

"Tell that to the boy in the street," he said lamely as she pressed her fingers against the loose fabric on his arm, sending a chill of excitement across his senses.

He was powerless against her—always had been. For as long as he could remember, she had been the red-haired woman of his dreams. Then she became the stuff of his waking nightmares. When she had relented to his glances and stares, he had blamed himself, and every night he paid the price. For the first year, in his dreams, his father strangled him in his bed. His tutor and father's closest friend Kratos killed him in numerous ways for a year or so after that. Sometimes, his father and Kratos both jointly killed him, plunging long knives into his chest for what he had been doing with his sister.

In some deep recess of his mind, Julian wanted to be punished. He knew that his relationship to his half-sister would never be truly accepted by his father. It wasn't just that she was blood. It did not expand the interests of the House of Mallory. Like death and murder, marriage must serve some lasting purpose.

Lord Janus Mallory had wanted Julian to marry a Vossen to secure the south. Maybe even the heir Jeremy, a strong fighter and friend to the crown. The banditry across the northern roads was nothing but a twisted but common type of game played by his father Janus. The monetary losses were intended to build up pressure over time to get Lord Vossen to the table, to make the commitment that would bond the southern kingdoms together.

But the Vossens had resisted Mallory marriages for centuries. Julian believed they would never relent; that the Vossens somehow knew of the cancer within the Mallory family. Maybe they had heard the rumors about his mother falling out of favor with his father, and Jaynah's mother a year before that. They had likely heard rumors of the liberties his father Janus had taken with some of the local nobles, women who only too gladly left their husbands for a weekend. Perhaps the Vossens even knew what Julian and Jayna had been doing all these years—that the scion of the Mallory line was in his sister's room right now.

She kissed him, and the world began to spin. She pulled him by the buttocks toward the bed, and he went only too willingly. Any memory of his nightmares was gone. There was only his lust and their chemistry.

"Quiet," she reminded him in his ear.

"I'm not the one who makes noises," he said.

She smiled and he breathed deeply, filling his nose with her natural musk that dulled his mind like she was the strongest alcohol in existence.

"Then help me, brother," she said as she grabbed his hand and brought it to her mouth. She gently bit his palm and pressed it against her face.

He left her room an hour or two later, but in the darkness, after they had both been spent multiple times, they cuddled and spoke of a world they knew would never exist. It was her dream, but it was one that they both shared. She lived in a house on the sea where she could live apart from her father. Two sons and a daughter played near a warm hearth.

Every night, in this dream, she lay the entire night on her crimson sheets nestled onto the chest of her beloved. He always squeezed her when she finished her story there, and then closed his eyes until the afterglow of his lover's dream and the warmth of her body against him washed away his worries. Then he left her bed like a thief in the night and hoped that the memory of her warmth was enough to get him through his terrors.

That night was no different. He hoped their liaison might calm his mind and help him forget. But the memory of her warmth was not enough to keep the screams of the villagers in Perketh out of his nightmares.

LORD VOSSEN'S RESPONSE

LORD EDWARD VOSSEN rubbed the bald patch on the top of his head as he sat forward in his wolf-hide leather chair, listening intently. He looked to his tall, armor-clad, brown-bearded son Jeremy frequently as the lanky man before him tumbled over each word, weaving a fantastical tale of banditry, necromancy, and treachery from his neighbor Lord Mallory.

"I mean no offense, Milord," the man with the matted brown hair croaked. "I was paid by Lord Mallory to raid your caravans. To kill your men. Honest. He paid, and I did the work."

The elder Vossen nodded. "And you stopped because an undead man killed your friends?"

"I tell you... the thing was unnatural!" the man stammered. "I put three arrows into him. Three arrows!"

"Perhaps you missed," Jeremy said from his rigid stance beside his father.

"I never miss!" the man said. "The arrows were sticking out of his chest. They call me the Archer. Perhaps you've heard of me? I'm a legend in the eastern wood!"

"Sure, you are," Jeremy said.

For the briefest moment, the man eyed the young lord dangerously, but the look was gone in seconds. He must have remembered why he was here—that he was begging Lord Vossen for protection from the necromancer and the retribution of Lord Mallory for leaving his post along the roads and forests.

"I've never seen a necromancer," Edward said, "never even heard of one outside of old fables."

"That's because they don't exist," Jeremy said.

"Two arrows were in the man's heart," the Archer said. "I tell you I never miss!"

"Perhaps he had armor," Jeremy said.

"Perhaps he died of his wounds later," Edward said.

The Archer shook his head. "He was completely unfazed by them. Lifted a boulder above him and smashed it through my friend's head, down through his shoulder blades. I've never seen anything like it. I've seen death... I've seen horrors... I've committed..."

Lord Edward raised his large eyebrows, waiting for the man to finish—to admit that some of those atrocities had been against Edward's own men.

"I'm done with that life now," the Archer said.

"Then what use do I have of you?" Lord Edward asked. "What possible purpose would I have of a mangy bandit in my keep? You want me to put you up in one of my kennels so you can lounge around with my dogs?"

"He has the smell of them," Jeremy said. "They'd probably assume he was one of them."

The Archer fretted with a bent old cap between his hands.

"There'd be upkeep for me though," Edward said. "I'd have to feed another mongrel."

"I could earn my keep," the Archer said earnestly. "I can hunt for you. I can hit a bird from a hundred paces."

"I don't need birds," Edward said, "and I have my own huntsmen. Are you saying my huntsmen are deficient?"

"N-n-n-o, Milord," the Archer said, bowing and nearly falling all over himself. "I mean how would I know? I only mean to be of service. I could chop wood."

"I have my own woodcutters."

"Can you sing?" Jeremy asked with a smirk on his face.

The Archer panicked as he massaged his throat. Edward thought he might try to belt out a tune, but the man shook his head instead.

"Then what good are you?" Jeremy asked, unsheathing his sword with a twang and marching so quickly toward the man that this Archer character fell over in fear.

"Please!" the Archer begged. "I'll do whatever you want! Just don't send me back into the eastern wood!"

Lord Edward rubbed his head, thinking of his options. The King had paid off the ransom to Lord Mallory, and Edward expected the banditry of his tax payments to Eldenwald to cease immediately. He wondered if this entreaty was just another Mallory trick. He fumed inwardly, seething at Mallory's games and the way he had manipulated Edward's defense of the southern border from orcish incursion.

He wanted to repay the treachery on Lord Mallory with something big—something that would teach Mallory to never play another game with him or his family again. Where Mallory had used small parties of bandits, Edward would send a much larger force to teach a bigger lesson. He couldn't send an army of knights, pikemen, and archers because King Eldenwald would undoubtedly interfere to keep the peace. He needed an army, but one that could not be so easily traced to himself. What he needed was an army of derelicts. Bandits. Archers.

"I have something for you," Edward said, "a task for which I believe your history and talents are more suited to than chopping wood or lying with dogs."

"Milord?" the Archer asked.

"Your friends that were killed. I assume they weren't your only friends."

The Archer shrugged, oblivious.

"You have other friends somewhere," Edward said, "other bandits that you can pass orders to."

"Bandits aren't very good at following orders," the Archer said. "I mean no offense, Milord, but we vagrants are defined by a sort of rebellious spirit…"

"Payments then," Edward said. "Other bandits that you can pass payments to…"

"Aye," the Archer said. "Coin'll move 'em."

"How many such friends do you have?" Jeremy asked.

Edward smiled at the thought of how effortlessly his son understood him. He was proud.

"How much money do you plan on passing out?" the Archer asked. "I've noticed that the more money I have, the more friends I tend to gather."

"Friends are like that," Edward agreed. "I'm looking for about 500 friends."

"That's not a group of friends," the Archer said, still not completely catching on or maybe just acting more shrewdly than was necessary. "That's an army."

"Indeed," Edward said. "I need an army. Loyal to me but not bannered. Willing to do what needs to be done."

"Done to what?" the Archer asked.

"Not what," Jeremy said, "to whom."

Edward continued smiling under his hands as he nodded to his son.

"You'll have food," Edward said. "You'll find shelter if you need to fall back to my lands. You'll lead your men to each town—"

"Milord," the Archer interrupted. "I'm afraid I'm not much of a leader. I can spread the word, as discreetly as I can. I think I can get the men, but keeping them in line is not… how I work, I guess. I tend to stick to a plan, string up my bow, and aim it at what needs shooting."

Edward nodded in understanding. He needed someone he could trust to lead these vagabonds anyway—someone to keep the pillaging and raping in check enough to keep the King out of his business. He folded his arms across his blue doublet and looked at his son. Jeremy nodded.

"You can't wear your armor," Edward said.

"I know," Jeremy replied.

"No one can recognize you."

"I'll keep my distance," Jeremy promised. "If Lord Mallory sees me up close, he'll know me. He has sought me out at parties, asked me if I favor his daughter."

Edward guffawed. "That chance!"

"Nonetheless," Jeremy said, "I could paint my face, keep my helmet on and remove my colors."

"You don't have to be out front," Edward reminded him. "Perhaps you should bring someone you trust, someone who can keep you out of the limelight and advise you. We could delay a couple of days for you to seek out Freddie in the capital."

"He's a black-and-white kind of guy," Jeremy said. "He'd be more likely to report us than help us. Besides, he's on a secret assignment."

"Secret assignment?" Edward asked. "What secret assignment?"

"He was recently promoted. The King sent him on a mission."

"Ah," Lord Edward said, "probably scouting the Southern Peaks for orcish incursions. He's always been the type to seek out adventures. Well, you know what to do. If someone notices you, kill them. This isn't something a Vossen can be found doing."

"I understand," Jeremy said, grunting in acknowledgement. "Bribery would only last so long. A loose tongue must be cut out."

Edward nodded in agreement and smiled at the Archer, who appeared to grasp the implications all too well. It wasn't his son Jeremy's style to not lead the charges, but this incursion was not the stuff of songs and legends. Whoever led this raid would be known in infamy. His son must be anonymous and only leading from the shadows. The evil must be named elsewhere. The Devil's Archer, perhaps.

"I want every town between our keep and Mallory's burned to the ground. I want you to take this *Archer*'s friends to the very gates of Mallory's base of power, and I want you to burn an image of our might into that land's memory."

"But Milord," Archer said. "Mallory is a malicious man. He is unlikely to learn a lesson from you killing his subjects."

"The lesson is not just for Mallory," Jeremy said. "It's for the commoners. If such actions happen again, it will not be a Mallory that suffers. It will be the families of the bandits. It will be the families of everyone who knew the bandits."

"You will pillage your countrymen," Edward said to the Archer. "You will sow fear. You will rape. You will murder. In short, you will do those many things to which you have grown accustomed."

"But I—"

"And if you don't," Edward said, "or if any harm comes to my son after he steps foot in Mallory's lands, I will bring down the wrath of the titans on everyone you've ever known. You will feel my wrath. Your family will be wiped from existence. Everyone who has ever met your family will taste their own blood in their mouths."

"Yes, Milord."

"It will be done," Jeremy agreed.

"And..." the Archer said squeakily, "we'll be paid?"

Lord Vossen let out a hearty laugh. "Take this man to the treasury. See that he gets his purse filled. And hand him as many purses as he needs to pay his *friends*."

Jeremy nodded. He started to walk out but Edward grabbed him by his vambrace.

"Make sure Lord Mallory gets my lesson," Edward said. "Janus plays with toy soldiers. We play with armies."

Jeremy walked through the door from the main admittance hall. The haggard Archer followed him, bowing to Edward and offering his thanks and praise.

Edward placed his chin against his fist and imagined a fire that stretched from his property line all the way to Mallory Keep. He smiled widely and genuinely before closing his eyes and leaning back into the wolf-hide leather chair.

THE BANDIT INCURSION

FREDERICK ROSS RODE on a prized white steed, a gift from his father Godfrey after being promoted to Captain—the third captain in the Ross family in the past three generations. Along with the war stallion, he had been given a new set of steel armor with curved armaments meant to deflect most long arrows that glanced and didn't hit center mass. He wore a high white plume of feathers, in the style of his family, and his visor was up, revealing his manicured goatee with long mustache flare-out and strands of blond hair.

Frederick was on loan to Lord Mallory from the capital, a part of the payment provided to end the hostilities between Vossen and Mallory over travel costs in the last orcish incursion. Frederick had only been promoted to Captain a few months prior, and Godfrey had been immensely proud. A feast had been held in his son Frederick's honor, and his father embarrassed him with accolades and boasts that his eldest son would outdo even the storied history of Lord General Godfrey Ross, hero of multiple orcish aggressions.

In truth, Frederick had only excelled in administrative and training tasks in the military so far, earning top marks for the small but effective ways he had managed his assignments. He was eager to prove to his father and the world that these accolades might be in some small way true. He eagerly yearned for battle, outside of the relative safety of tournaments, in which he was a champion several times over.

When news broke out in the Mallory Keep that a bandit force had begun pillaging the western border of the Mallory territory, Frederick had volunteered and suggested a small reconnaissance force. The men he led were mostly Mallory regulars in chain mail, all personally vouched for by the Mallory master at arms. Nine men, not counting himself, and all accomplished horse riders. Two archers brought up the rear, and he led from the front, like his father.

As he rode atop a hill south of Perketh, near Dona, a small column of smoke could be seen rising from the west. He stopped his horse Lightning and waited for his men to catch up.

"You think it's them?" a knight named Simon asked.

Frederick nodded as he surveilled the field ahead of them. If they moved straight toward the smoke, they were a bit exposed on the approach to the wood. He pointed along the backside of the hill and waved his hand in a 90 degree angle indicating the group should enter the wood along the crest and work their way through the forest. Simon nodded and passed the order down the line.

Frederick again led the way at a canter, eyeing the forest warily. Birds chirped and the breeze carried the smell of charred timber to them. He lowered his visor, ready for combat. He checked behind him and found the others in varying degrees of preparedness.

"Take this seriously," Frederick commanded. "We have reports that there are dozens of bandits working together."

"Sir," an archer said, "we go into these woods and we'll have little to no warning if we encounter anyone in mass."

"Agreed," he replied, "but if we go across that field, we could be walking into a hail of arrows. I'm the best armored here, but if I move against 20 arrows, I'm more likely to meet one that finds me disagreeable. Besides, I like my horse."

The men chuckled.

"Bandit groups are usually small," Simon said from the Captain's right. "I've never seen more than five or six at a time. I've never heard of anything like this ever happening before. Bandits don't just form militias."

"They have some claim against Lord Mallory," Frederick said. "The word we have from scouts is they call themselves the Red Army. I've heard they have a red flag and fashion themselves with red sashes."

"What do you think they want?" Simon asked.

"What does any bandit want?" Frederick answered rhetorically. "Your sack of gold, your food and whatever else you might have on you. Maybe your life."

"Sure," Simon said, "but bandits don't need an army for that. They're opportunists. They rely on the element of surprise. What do they want? This doesn't add up."

"Perhaps if you come across one, you can ask him…"

Simon chuckled.

As they worked their way slowly along the tree line, Frederick noticed movement in the grove ahead. He motioned for his two archers and Simon to accompany him while the other six men guarded the horses. He moved cautiously with his well-oiled gear along the bare ground and grass where possible, avoiding leaves whenever he could. Ahead, a small commotion rose from two men encamped at the edge of the small forest outside of Perketh.

"You think Mallory will send anyone?" a man asked his companion. Between both of them were two bows and quivers of arrows leaning against a massive, tall maple tree.

"Eventually," the brown-haired companion said. "The boss man says we should expect a few scout parties first."

"You mean knights?"

"Maybe," the companion said.

"I've always wanted to prick a knight," the man said, pointing at his bow sitting next to a tree.

"Perhaps you'll get your chance soon," the companion said, nodding and picking at his teeth with a green blade of long grass.

Frederick motioned toward one of his archers, pointed at the man who had talked about killing a knight, and then made a cutting motion across his throat. He pointed at the other archer and made a drawn bow motion and finger-walking toward the group. Both archers nodded and Frederick and Simon drew longswords.

Frederick held up three fingers. Then two. Then one. When his fist closed, a bow twanged and an arrow shot across the eighty feet or so between them, burying itself in the middle of the man's chest. Frederick and his men burst out of the wood and his other archer let loose an arrow that buried itself into the remaining man's hand as he reached for his bow.

The man screamed in agony and rolled onto the ground.

Frederick grabbed the bandit by the shoulder and rammed him into the tree.

"Are you part of the Red Army?"

"Of course not!" the man tried to lie as he covered his red sash with his free hand. "I was just sitting—"

"We heard you talking about Lord Mallory," Frederick hissed. "Who sent you here? What grievance do you have with Lord Mallory? I'm from Kingarth. Tell me what grievance your people have, and I might find audience with the King. I can help."

The man chuckled.

"Oh, right," the man said, favoring his arrowed hand. "I'm sure you would, and I guess you'd just march right through the Red Army to do it, would you? I don't need your pity. We make our own way. We don't need you lords..."

"Oh, sure!" Simon said. "Real strong men, you lot are! How many women and children have you pushed around today?"

"We're two hundred strong," the man bragged. "And we're growing. The call has gone out. More come in every day. Perketh is burning, little lords, and there's nothing you can do to stop what's coming!"

Frederick checked the woods for more movement, but all he could hear were the birds and the rustling of branches and leaves in the wind.

"So, your target is Perketh?" Simon asked.

"Our target isn't one town," the man said. "We're plundering the whole territory. We have grievances, we do! Taxed out of our homes to fund some war poem for a stupid lord and his crotch lice! I hope the whole lot of you burn."

Frederick drew a knife from his belt. He rested it in his hand, sideways, poised for a slice. He positioned himself so effortlessly that the threat didn't seem to register to the cornered man. Simon joined him in holding the man against the trunk.

"Last question," Frederick said. "Where's your leader?"

The man laughed. "Where would you be? Perketh is burning, *milord*! Why don't you go admire the flames?"

Frederick's wrist flicked fast as lightning across the man's neck, leaving a grizzly red stain that spread in the afternoon sun. The man's lips moved, likely trying to tell some jibe at Frederick's expense. It wasn't until the sound of air came out of his neck that realization dawned on the man's face. He panicked and flailed against their hold. Wet sticky blood poured down the man's brown shirt and red sash. They held him there as he bled out and didn't release him until he stopped gurgling and spasming.

"That's a cold way to go," Simon said as he let go of the man.

"I hate bandits," Frederick said, "and if Perketh has really been sacked, then these men are lower than low. Anyone who preys on the weak and the women and children deserves a long death—one filled with agony, pain, and panic."

"Still," Simon said, "bad way to go."

Frederick kicked the leg of the other bandit who still leaned against the tree. The man never even reached for the arrow in his chest. The strike was instantly fatal.

"My only regret," Frederick said, "is that our archer friend here was too good a marksman. This one should have died more slowly."

"I'll keep that in mind, Captain," the archer said with a smile.

Frederick clapped the archer on the shoulder. He and his three men returned to their horses and made their way toward the smoke and the distant screaming. A cacophony of metal, hooves and cries drowned out the sounds of their own footsteps. They moved in a circuitous route south and found five men with red sashes raping a woman along the road from Shirun to Perketh. Two men held down her arms as their cohorts cheered on a man who was vigorously thrusting and spitting in the woman's face as she fought against the hands that pinned her down.

Two arrows split the heads of the spectators, and Frederick leapt from his horse with his sword at the ready. He plunged it through the rapist's chest cavity, spreading blood all over the poor woman and the wagon on which she was pinned.

"I'm sorry," Frederick said lamely as he realized he should have thought of the blood spray.

The two remaining men screamed and released her and ran toward the western woods. Simon and the two archers gave chase. Frederick didn't have to watch them. He knew his archers would catch the perpetrators if his squires didn't. His four other men stood ready, encircling him.

He knocked his visor up and absently stroked the plume atop his helmet. It was a nervous tick of his that happened when he couldn't think of something to say. The woman looked in shock and disbelief at the blood all over her body.

"I should have gotten him off you first," Frederick apologized. "I wasn't thinking."

She guffawed queerly as she pushed her dress back down and began to rub the blood all over her body. "No, good knight. This will do."

"Are you hurt?"

Her eyes tensed up. She groggily looked back at a small house some twenty yards away.

"I don't…" she said but nodding. "I don't feel anything."

Tears began to fall down her face. Frederick left her and moved to the fence and saw two sets of small legs from behind a wheelbarrow. The boys didn't move. As he approached, he covered his gaping mouth with his hand. Their innards had been cut from them, likely in front of the mother. The children had been dragged around the yard. Blood was everywhere. Madness and evil had been here.

Frederick gripped his sword and gritted his teeth. He strode to the woman. He pointed to the dead bandits beside her.

"Bathe in their blood if you like," he said. "If it provides you some comfort, I'll empty the others onto you as well. Say the word and I'll bring back all the blood you require!"

She stared at her body, raising her bloody hands in front of her face before looking back at him. "It would be an empty thing… Like me, I feel. Unnecessary… without purpose…"

"Is your husband also?"

She laughed so hard she cried, as she rolled off the wagon and began shuffling back toward her house and the backyard that held her horrors. "He left us long ago. For all I know, he's one of these men… this Red Army."

"I'll tell the King of your loss," Frederick promised. "I'll petition for grievances."

"I have grief enough," she said softly.

"At least tell me your name," the Captain said.

"Sarah," she said. "Sarah Crow."

"I'll…" he said, trying to think of some promise to her. A song sounded too flippant. He would offer her a rose, but this wasn't a tournament. What she had suffered was loss beyond what he could comprehend in the moment. "I'll kill as many of them as I can."

She turned to him along the short, barren path, likely trampled by her boys in their young years. She nodded as more tears fell.

"Yes," she said. "Please."

He leapt atop Lightning and Simon followed him closely on his own mount. They found a bandit group and slayed seven more before any backup arrived. Frederick became wraithlike, solely focused on carnage for Sarah. In his mind, he saw each of these men killing the small boys at the house on the road to Shirun, and they all paid bloodily for the damage they had inflicted.

Ten more on the road leading to Perketh. Five more in the forests just south of the smoke. Three more who had made camp and offended his ears with their boasts of rapes and murders. A small group of six who managed to ding his armor with arrows before he ripped their insides from their stomachs and spat into their faces as the light faded from their eyes.

Covered in their blood, he meandered through the wood, hoping against hope that Perketh still stood—that he had made it in time to save even one of these people. But the screams were muted and the smoke was beginning to subside, as if there wasn't much more to burn.

He stumbled through the trees until he came to a shadow there, watching the town. Unlike the faceless men he had slaughtered, this one seemed familiar. Frederick raised his visor, squinting at the leather-clad, brown-bearded man in a long leather cap and non-descript armor who had not noticed his approach.

"Jeremy?" Frederick asked, surprised.

He knew Jeremy Vossen from anywhere. They had enjoyed many a strong ale together in the capital. Jeremy had even served as wingman to him while table hopping at social events, often distracting fathers as Frederick had stolen a kiss from Lucille Croft, Evelyn Crayton and any number of other dangerous potential liaisons.

"Freddie?"

Frederick forgot himself. He almost forgot where he was, as if the mayhem and retribution had all been a dream and this chance meeting was the reality. He took his helmet off and smiled widely and genuinely through his twirled blond mustache. He stroked the plume of his helmet as he thought of something to say.

"Lord Vossen has sent you here, hasn't he?" Frederick asked, walking up to him and giving him a hug.

"Yeah…"

The hug was returned but lighter and stiffer than usual.

"Well, I'm so glad you're here," Frederick said. "I'm only leading ten men, but they're good men. We've killed dozens. Maybe three. I haven't been counting. But man, we could use you."

Jeremy nodded, but he seemed lost.

"You ok?" Frederick finally asked.

"You're on loan," Jeremy said, in a rambling sort of way. "The King loaned you to Mallory over the repayment, didn't he? This was your special assignment?"

"Yeah," Frederick said with laughter still in his voice at seeing his old friend. "I thought it would be a quiet time on the frontier. I expected I'd be patrolling orcish borders, not this…"

He motioned at the smoke and bodies he had left in his wake.

"Whatever this is!" he said finally. "Man, I have some stories to tell you the next time we sit down…"

"I bet…" Jeremy said, hugging him again.

Frederick patted Jeremy on the back, slightly confused.

"There was this woman," Frederick said. "Sarah. I found men… pinning her down. They were… You know… I… We killed them all, but not before they had killed her boys. Spread them out all over her yard… I left her there…"

He winced as he thought about her covered in blood, turning toward him on the path to her small home and the graves she would have to dig.

"I wish you hadn't come," Jeremy said, grabbing him by the back of the neck.

"No one wants to be here," Frederick said, smiling at his friend, "but someone had to come. It's a good thing I came. That we both came! You and me together? The Red Army doesn't stand a chance!"

A sharp pain pierced Frederick's neck and a metal taste flooded his mouth. He gasped as he pushed away from Jeremy. He grasped around at his exposed neck and felt the knife handle. He fell to the ground.

"I wish you hadn't come," Jeremy said as he bent down to Frederick's level.

Every inhalation sent blood into his lungs. His body spasmed violently as he gasped for air. He reached out to Jeremy, who held his hand as he sputtered the last breath of his short 22 years. He looked up at the sky and thought of the tournaments he had won. Of his father's proud face in the crowd. Of Jeremy standing next to Godfrey and just as happy as he had been.

"God damn it, Freddie," Jeremy said. "God damn it…"

A SIGHT FOR SORE EYES

SIMON CASTERBY WATCHED in horror from the bushes as a man stood over Captain Ross. Frederick's final spasms had been grotesque and pained, but there was an agony there too in the brooding man.

"I will leave this place," the man with the brown beard said, now hunching down near Captain Ross' head. "I am done here. This army is without form and evil. They scatter like vultures to pick at the dead, forgetting their mission and thinking only of themselves. There is no order, and I cannot lead them. I have failed in my father's task. These men will loot and pillage endlessly until someone like you kills them all."

The man put his head in his hands. "But it can't be you now that you've seen me, and who else would it be? You didn't deserve this, Freddie. Neither did these people. My father was wrong to send me here. Gods, why couldn't you have been assigned anywhere else?"

The man shook his head, wiping tears from his eyes.

"I'll not bury you here in an unmarked grave," the man promised, still talking to Captain Ross. "I'll find a wagon, and I'll have Lightning pull you back to the capital. I'll be there every step of the way. I'll present you to Godfrey… I'll…"

The man didn't say another word. He seemed lost in thought, and Simon thought about charging the killer. But something told him to stay his hand, that this man may be more capable than he looked.

Simon had watched the man bury a knife into his Captain's throat. He had watched the man's reaction as Frederick's eyes had grown wider, and he began to clasp at his throat. His Captain had not just lifted his visor to greet this man. He had taken off his helmet, exposing his neck. This killer was a knight, possibly even a lord.

This was a man who Frederick knew well, and Simon knew a game that was above his head when he saw it. Simon was a knight in name only, with only the smallest of lands and titles to his family name. The Ross family was legendary. Ten Captains of the Royal Guard. Three continuous successions of Captain within their family in the past sixty years, and Frederick would have attained major and colonel ranks within five years. Simon was sure of it. He had fought like a madman, running headfirst into archer formations and turning his body with such expert care that two steel-tipped arrows had careened off that might have hit Simon in the chest, piercing right to the heart.

And yet, despite his skill and obvious training, Frederick lay dead and Simon still breathed. His mind tried to force a lesson onto itself. Never take your helmet off. Never trust a lord. Never trust a friend. No good deed goes unpunished. Each successive lesson more terrible than the previous one.

He followed the man from a safe distance and watched him follow through on his promises to Captain Ross. First, he found Lightning. Then, he requisitioned a cart that had not been burned. He hefted Frederick's body onto the flat wood flooring, and smacked the white horse on the rear to get him trotting. The horse looked back frequently, seeming to mourn his master in his own way. The man refused to mount the horse but instead walked alongside the cart, staring into the dead eyes of the man who seemed so destined for greatness.

Simon ran back to his squad to report the death of Captain Ross. Each hung their head low and cursed themselves for falling behind, but he knew it was not their fault. Captain Ross had lived his life like a true hero, charging into scores of men. Simon didn't tell the men how Frederick died. He left out the tale of the bearded man. All he told them was that Captain Ross had been stabbed in the neck, and a knight was bringing the Captain's body back to the capital.

With the bearded man heading toward Kingarth to tell his side of the story, Simon knew there was only one place he could tell his. He beckoned the men to follow him down the road through Dona, the one that led to Mallory Keep.

11

THE REBIRTH OF PERKETH

THE SCENT OF burning wood and flesh flooded
Ashton's nostrils on the road north from Mallory
Keep. At first, he thought he was hallucinating Riley's
death in Perketh Square. As he got closer to Perketh, he realized that he was not just torturing himself again. There really
was smoke and death nearby.

Clayton and he passed village after village, always finding the same scene of death and destruction. Depravity was
everywhere, and it preyed on the weak and defenseless. Naked
women lay along the main road. Old men had been beaten
and worse. Babies cried everywhere, except where they had
been thrown from windows onto the streets. A savage evil had
ransacked the city, and none were safe.

Everyone had been butchered. No regular army or militia
was in sight. No lightning bolts from the sky. Even the gods
must have been turning a blind eye.

Ashton threw up more than once at the inhumanity of

these men who ignored Clayton and him as they stumbled along the main roads. The bandits were too busy looting and raping in these villages to be bothered. When they were stupid enough to accost the two friends, it was the last thing they ever did. A man with a crooked knife and three friends approached them and demanded money a few miles south of Perketh. Clayton ripped off both of the man's arms and beat one of the bandit's accomplices to death with them. The third man ran off screaming.

"Go on," Ashton called after him. "Tell your shit friends!"

They reached Perketh mid-afternoon. The sun was beating down on them, baking the dead in the streets. Unfamiliar, half-charred brick and stone buildings greeted them around every corner. A few roofs in the town remained untouched, but for the most part, it was an alien, surreal homecoming. Without really thinking about his destination, Ashton's feet led him to Perketh Square, what was left of it.

With every step, he felt like people were staring at him, but the windows of the town were empty. He could smell the death, and in his bones, he could feel the loss. Every friend he had known. Every distant cousin and person who had attended Clayton's funeral.

Riley was still there. Someone had rammed sticks into her sides, desecrating her body—likely bandits who seemed numb to the pain and suffering of others and who didn't respect the dead. Not that the people of the town had been any better. They had burned her alive and left her here as a lesson. Don't commit witchcraft. Don't be a necromancer. Don't be Ashton.

Clayton nudged him, bumping his arm against Ashton's shoulder.

"What is it?" Ashton asked, staring into the blackened flesh of Clayton's wife.

He mumbled a response.

"I can't understand you."

"Bren back."

"Bren back?"

Clayton pointed at her and then back at himself. "Bren 'er back."

"Bring her back?"

Clayton nodded.

"Clayton, buddy," Ashton said. "I don't even know how I brought you back."

"Repit," Clayton said, clutching his jaw with his hand to try to speak better. "Do same."

"I don't know how I did it," Ashton said. "I was at your grave. I was crying. I wanted you to come back. I asked you to come back."

Clayton nodded. "Repit."

"I don't know if I can do it," Ashton said. "Besides, look at her."

Parts of her skin were untouched by fire, but her clothing had obviously taken to torch, and her breasts had melted down her stomach. Her hair was singed, and her eyes were glazed over and sunken. Still, a part of him wondered if she was waiting for him to bring her back like Clayton must have been.

"Try," Clayton said clearly. "Repit."

Ashton nodded. "For you," he said, "I'll try."

He readied himself in front of Riley, trying to remember exactly how he resurrected Clayton. "Do you think we need to bury her?"

Clayton shrugged.

Ashton felt embarrassed, like he had said something really stupid in front of a crowd—like hundreds of eyes were watching him, judging him.

"I was hovering over you," Ashton said, shaking the sense of being watched even though no bandits were around. "I begged you to come back to me and Riley."

Clayton unbound her hands from the stake and gingerly placed her on the stone tiles in the main square, away from the pyre she had been burned at. Her skin came off easily. Clayton patted the crispy skin back down. He nodded to his friend and motioned for Ashton to continue.

"Ok," Ashton said as he crawled beside her. "Ok, I'm doing it."

He tried to close her eyelids with his hand, but they were melted to the rest of her skin. He looked at her grotesque orbs and climbed atop her. He expected the smell to be overwhelming, but the rest of the sun-scorched bodies must have numbed his sense of smell or perhaps she had been in the square for too long. Perhaps it was too late.

"Repit," Clayton urged him again.

"Ok," Ashton said, waving a hand at him. "Let me concentrate. I think I need to talk to her like I talked to you."

Clayton nodded and folded his arms as he paced the stone square.

"Riley," Ashton said. "I know it's been a while. I'm sorry that Clayton and I left you here. It's been a couple weeks. We were... overcome with grief. Clayton misses you. I miss you too. We want to take you away from here—somewhere far away where we can all be together.

He placed a hand lightly against her flaking, crackling shoulder.

"We need you to come back to us."

He half expected her to bat her eyes and rustle beneath him, but she didn't.

"Clayton and I need you to come back to us," Ashton said. "You weren't supposed to die here… Return to us from the underworld, away from all that death and darkness. Come back to us. Come back to the light."

There was no response. The sense of being watched came back in full force. He looked around briefly, expecting bandits or refugees from the woods, but he and Clayton were alone. A board in a nearby building fell, likely weakened by the day's fire. A slight breeze rustled leaves somewhere behind him. Birds chirped in the distance.

"Come back to me," Ashton said. "I need you here. Clayton needs you here."

His senses seemed to focus on everything but her in his periphery. Something rustled in a building. Ashton became aware of footsteps approaching him. A wounded dog or something crawled along the stone steps of Mayor Seth's office, slithering down. He refused to look at or acknowledge their presence, and he cursed his brain for not focusing harder.

"It's just you, me and Clayton," he said. "Don't worry about them. They don't care about necromancy. There are bigger problems in the world. They're not burning me here like they did you. Clayton and I won't let them. Come back to me. Come back to me, Riley. Come back."

More footsteps approached him.

"Keep them away from me, Clayton," Ashton said,

waving his hand absently toward the noises. "Make sure they don't come back."

Clayton grunted an acknowledgement, but he didn't move.

"Come back," Ashton asked her again. He pushed against her chest with a finger, hoping she might respond to his antagonism from the afterlife. "Don't leave Clayton here by himself. Join us. Come back to us, if only for a moment. Help us avenge Perketh. Help us hide from those who might seek to harm Clayton and me. Protect us. Come back…"

He tried to raise her for thirty more minutes, never looking at the gathering audience around him. They didn't matter. No one jeered him. The bandits or townsfolk near him were silent, probably intimidated by Clayton.

"I don't think it's working," Ashton said finally. "I think she's too far gone… I had those blue stones from Farmer Albertson's fields. You know? The leylines or whatever. Maybe we should grab some of those and try again—"

He looked up. He expected to see bandits and dogs, but if they were among the crowd, they were changed. The people swayed there, waiting for something. Men, women and children, all mangled and deformed. Dead. Undead.

He recognized Mr. Merkins. Then Mrs. Selena. In his desperation to raise Riley, he had managed to raise the entire town of Perketh.

"Maybe I don't need the stones from Farmer Albertson after all," Ashton said lamely.

Clayton shook his head in agreement at the negative.

A large man in a black smock with red stains down his sides looked down at Ashton from the front row. Even with the gaunt face and slashes across his cheek, Ashton recognized Master Nathan anywhere. A realization dawned on Ashton at that point. He realized that he didn't have to run anymore. He didn't understand what he had done, but he knew these people. Despite what they had done to Riley, they were his neighbors. Beneath their glassy eyes was recognition. They knew who he was, and something akin to love was still there—just as it had been with Clayton when he had come back from the grave. Ashton knew, somehow, that they would fight to their end for him.

"Umm…" Ashton said, as they waited for him to say something. He stumbled through thoughts in his head. Finally, he held onto his friend Clayton and looked out at them.

"I'm sorry this happened to you," Ashton said. "I can't make this right. You'll never be the same, and I don't know how long any of you will last here amongst the world of the living. The only thing I can offer you, the only thing within my power to give you, is justice."

A low murmur built among the undead residents of Perketh.

"The bandits are moving east, and then I think they're going to move south toward Mallory Keep. There are many of them, but we are many as well."

There were people nodding in the crowd.

"You've already died once before," he said. "You died trembling in your homes. You died because you didn't fight together. You died alone, by yourselves, with your families—hoping for mercy. The time for fighting alone and begging for mercy ends today. We'll fight together now."

The crowd cheered again.

"Follow me to Mallory Keep," Ashton said. "Follow me and take vengeance on the Red Army!"

Nathan shouted louder than most, but the five hundred

reborn residents of Perketh each gave a shrill battle cry that echoed across the stone tiles in the main square and against the brick and mortar of the burned out buildings.

Caught up in the crowd's enthusiasm, Ashton began to leave Perketh, but Clayton wouldn't let him. He pointed at Riley on the stone tiles and then at the graveyard. Ashton felt immediately terrible at having forgotten about her.

He commanded the undead horde to exhume Clayton's old grave. Four large men gently lowered her down into the freshly dug pit, and the town participated in another funeral procession, much like they had for Clayton before. Clayton sat across from Ashton, where Riley had sat previously.

This time, the undead men and women of Perketh stooped to kiss Clayton's cheek. This time, the spouse of the buried wasn't the only one who looked ghoulish. The people's faces were just as gaunt as before but without makeup. Every person who bent down to kiss Clayton's cheek left marks of blood and ooze from their own wounds.

As the crowd waited at the edge of the wood to the south, Clayton and Ashton looked at each other.

"It's time," Ashton said.

Clayton patted the mound of earth that housed Riley's resting body. He grabbed three morning glories from a vine that had overgrown a nearby tombstone and laid them on her grave.

"Sleep well," Ashton told her from beside his friend. "We love you."

Clayton nodded and hugged the mound. In town, on the southern path to Mallory Keep, the people of Perketh waited. For Clayton to finish saying goodbye. For Ashton to lead them to their promised vengeance.

A Tale of the Fallen

LORD GODFREY WROTE a quick note in his daily journal about the mundane details of the Royal Guard, its status, and routine. No casualties. No sicknesses. Perfect bill of health for the regiment, minus the units on loan to the various prefectures of the realm. He thought of his son in Lord Mallory's lands as he dictated the time left on the loans of Royal Guardsmen into his parchment. At the end of the day, he'd bind these pages as he had done every day for thirty years.

He looked up from his menial tasks to find his aide-de-camp Gerard Bastille awkwardly standing before him. Gerard was a battle-tested, seasoned soldier. Awkwardness and being tongue-tied were unusual for him—Godfrey wouldn't have accepted him as an aide otherwise. Gerard was being trained as a potential replacement, even if his oldest son Frederick was assumed to be next in line.

"What is it?" Godfrey asked.

Gerard adjusted his greaves and then his shoulder armor.

"It's your son," Gerard said.

"My son?"

Godfrey laid the scrolls down and placed the pen atop them.

"And?" he asked finally.

"I'm not sure how to tell you this…"

"Has there been an accident?"

"No, General. I don't think so."

"Is my son here? In the capital?"

Gerard's eyes batted feverishly and he coughed lightly. "Yes, Sir."

"Has he come to ask to be reassigned?" Godfrey asked with some relief.

"No, Sir."

"What does he want?" Godfrey said gruffly as he rose to his feet.

Gerard bit his lip. "He wants for nothing. Sir, your son has been—"

Godfrey felt the room spin. Gerard said something else. It sounded like "killed", but in truth, Godfrey's mind had turned off. Gerard's voice droned on muted and ambient while other noises amplified. He became aware of the crackle of embers in the hearth of his office. The creaking and clanking of Gerard's armor resonated like an anchor being dragged along an iron girder. He swore he could hear a mouse farting in the wall.

"Show me his body," he said finally.

"Captain," Gerard said, "his body has only just arrived. Lord Vossen brought it here as soon as he found Frederick on the field south of Perketh."

"He died fighting the Red Army?"

"It looks that way," Gerard said.

"Show me his body," Godfrey repeated. "I want to see my son."

Most memories are fleeting things. A single image might be all that a person can remember of a childhood friend, a vacation to a beach, or the scent of a first girlfriend.

Godfrey couldn't remember what his first wife looked like. She had died over twenty years ago. He couldn't remember how she smelled or what her favorite color was, but he loved her and remembered her fondly because she had given him Frederick—died during childbirth doing it.

Godfrey couldn't remember the exact moment he first picked up a sword, though he still felt excitement every time he heard the clang of a sword removed from his scabbard. He could remember a tree he had practiced against in his family yard, but he couldn't remember a single swing he had done there.

These were all things that Godfrey loved, and he had only fleeting reminders of them when he focused hard on them. Godfrey's memories of Frederick were different.

Godfrey had memorized whole days he had spent with his son. Every strand of hair and its position on that boy's head. The first time Frederick had come in second place at a tournament when he was just fourteen years old and fighting grown men. The way Frederick had leaned in his saddle as he pressed forward in the joust. The first time he had been caught in his room with a girl, and the surprising words that made their way out of Godfrey's mouth, "be careful," as he closed the door. The moment Frederick graduated from military academy, beaming a wide grin under that blond mustache at his father, and Godfrey tearing up. He remembered the salty tears draining down his face and into his mouth, a sensation that was repeating itself now.

The taste broke him from his melancholy. He realized he was mindlessly following Gerard down the stairs of the spire to the ground floor, towards his son's body. He wiped a sleeve against his cheek. He was wearing his leathers that cushioned his chest from the harder edges of his armor, but not the armor itself. He was dressed for leisure in his office.

Is this appropriate for seeing my son?

There was no suit appropriate for seeing his dead son. There was no proper moment. This was not supposed to happen.

Frederick was the finest soldier Godfrey had ever trained, even better than he was, and that had made Godfrey proud. Despite the last orcish incursion and the call-to-arms, Godfrey had held Frederick back in the capital to let him see how a war was actually conducted—the politics and the logistics, all important aspects for a future commander.

His son was smart and a prodigy with a blade, lance and armor. He had all the tools to win on the field and in the council chambers. He had the experience. He had the pedigree. Frederick had been groomed to be the greatest commander the Surdel Kingdom had ever known. He was the finest tournament champion Surdel had produced in two generations. And despite his gifts and the enormous efforts and privileges bestowed on him by a doting father, Frederick had died in the southern states fighting a second rate army of ragtag idiots, likely hired by Lord Vossen to attack Mallory over nothing.

"Wait," Godfrey said. "Did you say Lord Vossen brought my son in?"

"Yes, sir."

"The elder?"

"No," Gerard said. "Jeremy, his close friend."

"His best friend," Godfrey corrected him.

Since Jeremy had been so close to Frederick, he was similarly recorded in Godfrey's mind. The boy was trouble, but no more than Frederick had been with women and drinking. In truth, the two men had been made for each other. Both had won tournaments, though Jeremy never in the same tournaments that Frederick had competed in. Jeremy had always placed well.

Godfrey nodded. It was a relief that his son had been found and cared for by a close friend, someone Godfrey trusted.

He found Jeremy in the hospital wing, standing in front of the table that held his son. He could only see his boy's armor, the very set that Godfrey had commissioned for him, and the top of his golden head, where the curls fell down to the floor.

Jeremy did not look up. His face was dark, and he had been crying. Godfrey wiped his own face and hugged his son's best friend. Jeremy returned the hug hard and cried even harder.

"I'm glad you're here," Godfrey said, pulling away from him.

"I came as soon as I found him."

"Where did you find him?"

Jeremy grew silent for a moment as he sniffed and wiped at his eyes. "In a wood south of Perketh. I came upon him as he lay dying."

"You killed the man who did this?" Godfrey asked.

Jeremy shook his head slowly. "No... I think Freddie may have killed him... there in the forest..."

Godfrey pushed Jeremy gently aside to look at his son. The bandits had not desecrated his boy. Jeremy must have found him before they had had the chance. For that, he was eternally grateful. There was a puncture wound to the neck, obviously done at close quarters. Too big to be an arrow and not big enough to be a sword.

"Someone got close enough to him to stab him with a knife?" Godfrey asked in disbelief.

Jeremy didn't answer.

"This kind of blow shouldn't be possible," Godfrey said. "I helped design this suit of armor myself. The visor locks against a neck guard."

He looked to Jeremy for affirmation of the preposterousness of this death, but Jeremy's eyes were on the floor. He was still crying.

"Did he take his helmet off?" Godfrey asked. "Was he playing with that damned plume again? Did you find him without headgear and neck guard?"

Jeremy nodded. He seemed to be thinking. Remembering. "When I first saw him, he was without headgear. He had taken it off."

"Why?" Godfrey asked. "What possible reason? He knows better. He has been trained to never underestimate an enemy. Never!"

Godfrey remembered harsh lessons he had metered out himself to his son. Dozens of examples in their family courtyard during sparring, teaching him to never turn his back on an enemy and to always wear his armor when battle was near. Never to showboat. Never to grandstand. Quickly kill and move away to a new advantageous spot. Always meet a force with overwhelming power. Never show weakness. Never present a soft surface.

None of this added up.

"Did you see anything else?" Godfrey asked.

Jeremy shook his head free of a trance. "Perketh was burning. I think he was running toward it. You could always count on Jeremy to run toward danger. Always thinking of others. Always doing the right thing, no matter what the cost. He was a hero. He died a hero, killing dozens of bandits of the Red Army. He'll be remembered. I guarantee it. I'll commission statues... stories... songs... I'll—"

Godfrey choked on his tears and mucus, leaning heavily against the table and interrupting Jeremy's promises. He wailed at the absurdity of this ending for his marvelous son. He caressed his son's golden locks and brushed them with his fingers until he retreated to a corner of the dark room and cried as the memories of his boy flooded over him.

He looked up at the ceiling and thought of the tournaments Freddie had won. Of Freddie's beaming face on one of Godfrey's favorite horses, a lance held at the ready. Of Jeremy standing next to Frederick after their graduation from the war academy. Of the look he imagined on his wife Martha's face if she had lived to see any of hundreds of small or large accomplishments of their amazing son. Of the many accomplishments Freddie would never live to see.

"God damn it," Godfrey said, his face wet. "God damn it all..."

THE DARK KNIGHT OF THE WOOD

ASHTON WALKED ALONGSIDE the reanimated men and women of Perketh as they shuffled along the devastation left behind the Red Army. Miles of murders weighed down on him. Every new visited home was a fresh horror. Every new living room a bloody mess waiting for resurrection.

He paused on the road to Mallory Keep where a trail of blood led to a nearby house. He knew the family of seven whom had lived here. The man was a carpenter and he supported his wife and mother-in-law with their four children—three girls and a boy. It was the type of place that did not belong to a town or village. If someone asked where you lived, you simply said you lived between Perketh and Dona.

From the nearby woods, a horse whinnied. Ashton turned to find a man in dark black armor and a gold star cresting a horizon painted on his chest. His helmet was ornate with gold swirls and trim around the visor. On his back was a gold-and-steel war hammer. In his hand, a long, gray spear, likely used for jousting and charging.

"Where were you when they died?" Ashton yelled.

The knight surveyed the host around Ashton. He paced his horse along the side of the forest.

"Where were you?" the knight asked in response.

Ashton grumbled. He looked at the house where he knew more victims waited for him.

"Are you the necromancer?" the man hailed in a powerful, booming voice.

"Are you a Mallory man?"

The knight shook his head. "I belong to no man. I am pledged to… something else… to a greater power…"

"So you are with the King, then?" Ashton called.

The knight again shook his head.

"Are you here to kill the necromancer?" Ashton asked. "Is that why this *greater power* sent you?"

"I'm here to keep the peace."

"The peace?!" Ashton yelled. He pointed to the blood trail that led to the home of the carpenter. He pointed to the host of hundreds of dead innocents who walked along the path to Mallory Keep. "Does this look like peace to you?"

"I'm sorry for your loss," the knight said sincerely, "but they're not my charges."

"Do you not live here?" Ashton asked. "Are these not your people? What kind of lord are you?"

"I am no lord," the knight said, "and I live nowhere and everywhere. I'm not the type of man that the king rewards with lands. Those days have long passed."

Ashton mumbled to Clayton who eyed the well-armed

traveler warily. "Curse a man who speaks in riddles. We don't have time for this."

Ashton walked toward the house, following the trail of sticky blood that dripped slowly down the wooden stairs and pooled in the grass and mud. The carpenter Jerry, who Ashton had made a hammerhead for at Master Nathan's forge, lay face-first in the dirt, his cream-colored shirt stained with red. His wife Mary lay in a heap only ten feet away on the deck. She had been cut deeply across her throat. Ashton climbed the stairs, dreading the sight of the children. The girls had been violated and stacked on the kitchen table. Their small son Jeffrey still held a small knife where he sat in the kitchen. His eyes had been gouged out and a hilt protruded from his chest.

Ashton stumbled out of the house and slipped down the stairs. His stomach churned and he tasted bile. His hands fumbled along the carefully-crafted railing along the porch, the craftsmanship of a master carpenter, until he found a patch of grass that had not been touched by blood. He vomited there for a full minute. His head swooned from the heat and the nausea. Twice he thought he was done throwing up, but his stomach found something else to bring up.

He steadied himself against the railing.

"What kind of necromancer are you?" the knight called from the wood. "Squeamish at the first signs of death, when the smells are at their sweetest and the bodies have not yet bloated? What happens when you must walk beside a corpse who has been decaying for months?"

Ashton snarled. "This is not the path I chose!" he yelled back at the man in the dark armor with the gold star. "I am not here for the dead! I am here for the living!"

He trudged through the blood to look at Mary and Jerry.

Again, he felt a strong presence here—like the family were still present, watching him. But Mary's eyes were glossy and a gray film was over them.

Clayton put his hand on Ashton's shoulder, comforting him. Ashton put his hand on his friend's.

"If the knights of this land will not protect the people," Ashton said, "then we will…"

"I'm no knight," the man said from the edge of the forest.

"Then what do you do in all that armor?"

"I fight for the people too," the man said. "In my own way, against an enemy that only someone such as I am equipped to deal with."

"The people are attacked by bandits," Ashton said, "but you wait for another enemy to appear?"

"I don't deserve your spite," the man said, pointing at the hundreds of maimed undead shuffling between them along the road. "I do have pity. I do see them suffer."

"The suffering of these people is over," Ashton said. "Save your pity for the living."

The man lowered his head and backed into the darkness of the woods.

"Remember the Rule of Three," the man in the black armor said, "and I will bother you no more…"

"The Rule of Three?" Ashton asked under his breath.

He turned back to the door. In his mind, he could almost see Jerry sitting on the porch with Mary, watching him. The ghosts of their daughters and son smiled and waved from the doorway. Somewhere in the backyard, Mary's mother wandered amongst the garden, probably judging Jerry for not fighting the bandits off.

Ashton closed his eyes.

"If you want vengeance," he said, "if you don't want your final act on this world to be the way you've died here, then I beg you to come back. Join me and your neighbors. Help us fight the Red Army. Stand with us before Lord Mallory. Make him answer for his neglect—for letting these men prey on us all like wolves…"

Mary was the first to stir. She stumbled down the stairs from the deck on her hands and feet. Ashton tried not to let on how creeped out he was by her strange movements. He smiled as welcoming as he could as she bowed briefly to him before pulling herself to her feet with the aid of the deck's railing. Ashton pointed toward the line of marchers, and she fell in behind a man with a mangled arm.

Jerry woke next. He walked up the stairs and leaned heavily against the door frame. He barked an order into the house, and Ashton heard the sound of soft bodies sloshing against the floor. Without seeing them, Ashton knew the children had woken.

Ashton turned toward the procession and fell in step with his people. He looked to the woods, but the man in the dark armor was gone.

Ashton pulled his brown hood and cloak down until it almost touched his nose. He brooded about the lake of blood in the house he just left. He thought about Riley's charred body in the Perketh Square. He closed his eyes as he imagined the dark carriage racing away from Clayton's body, along this same road to Mallory Keep.

As he marched, his dark thoughts ebbed. There was a strange calming effect about being in the mob. There was a sense of dread purpose here and of strength in numbers. He found himself swaying in the same manner as the undead, following the cadence of their lock step march. He felt their swelling anger, and he joined them in that too.

He looked at the shopkeepers and housewives. The masters and apprentices. The mothers and daughters. The fathers and sons. Ashton swore that their losses would not be in vain. It may cost him his life, but the Red Army would pay for their sins upon his people.

THE DEAD SOUVENIR

THE ARCHER, DE facto leader of the Red Army now that Jeremy Vossen had abandoned them, walked into a house on the outskirts of Dona, a town roughly seven miles north of Mallory Keep. The house was one of dozens he had entered that day, looking for loot. He cared not for the women, not like many of his men. He'd pay for a well-kept whore when he needed that relief.

His men had already visited this house. A woman lay dead in the kitchen, her blood draining through the loose gray boards to the cold, hard-packed ground below. The house had been mostly picked clean of whatever few trinkets and metal that had remained in this hovel of a home.

He came to the house for something else.

"He's out back," a grisly man named Murphy with a red sash and blood-stained brown tunic said.

The Archer grunted. He exited through a creaky door that was only attached at the bottom hinge and strode confidently down the stairs. A thigh-high gray wood fence with many loose boards surrounded the small yard. A simple clothes-line spanned the middle of the muddy field, blocking his view of most of a shed at the back of the property. A few blood curdling screams could be heard nearby where his men slaughtered another family. Closer still, the sound of thrusting from his men taking liberties. His eyes weren't on the rickety projects around him but the trail of blood from the steps to the shed.

"He turned tail," the grisly lieutenant behind him said. "Soon as we came through the door. Didn't have a lick o' fight in him."

"Sounds about right," Archer said.

"Frank caught him in the back," the man said. "He dragged himself yonder there. I knew you wanted to see him. That's why I sent Frank to find you."

Archer nodded as he pushed through the creamy sheet with the blood stain from where a hand had pushed it aside. His dark brown boots sloshed in the crimson mud along the stained ground.

"Where were you going, Karl?"

He pushed the door to the shed inward. Karl coughed, favoring his stomach as he lay on his side looking at Archer. A loose board had been disturbed near Karl's head, exposing a hole in the floorboards.

"How you doing, Stan?" Karl asked, feigning pleasant conversation.

"Is that where you hid it?" Stanley the Archer asked. "Has it been here all this time?"

Karl coughed on his blood. "Go to hell!"

Archer laughed. "If only you'd have had that much fight in

you at the dig… Did you run away like this when Sam needed you at Xhonia?

"Demons," Karl said. "Demons… killed your brother. Black… Came out of the hole. Hot breath. Claws… Fangs…"

"So, it's not your fault?" Archer asked mockingly. "You did everything you could."

"They were… eating us…"

"How did my brother die?"

"Not well… Not well at all…"

A tear welled in Archer's eye. He had raised Sam in the wilderness. The boy had only been sixteen. He had never been in love. He had never been out of the south. The kid never had a chance to really live.

"And you just took the loot and ran?" Archer asked.

"We broke something," Karl said before a fit of coughing. "What we took… You saw the ice recede before you left. Deep blue water, frozen there in the old city. Receded somewhere… into the darkness. After the ice left, the demons came. I took the device. It's here… Someone's going to need it. Someone who can fight."

Karl patted the loose board.

"I kept running south," Karl said, "returned home, but I was a shit father and a worse husband. I couldn't stop thinking… about them… I felt like the demons might come out of the ground, looking for it. So, I left them there to live a better life without me."

"Perketh is burned to the ground," Archer said. "Everyone you might have known there is dead."

"Margaret?"

"She's been gone for years."

"What about my son?"

"If he was in Perketh, he's joined her in the underworld."

Karl leaned back against the rickety wall.

"Don't give me no act!" the Archer said. "If you cared so much for either of them, you wouldn't have left. I mean, what brought you here? Fear? Is that what drove you to shack up with this woman? In this hovel?"

"She expected less of me," Karl said, "and this place was farther from Xhonia."

"You were on watch that night," Archer said. "I know because I set up the schedule. I had to report back to our sponsors. I trusted you to keep him alive."

"I couldn't," Karl said before spitting up blood. "They were demons, Stanley. They ripped him apart. It was over in seconds."

"I'm going to kill you now," the Archer said.

"Good," Karl said, steadying himself against the wall. "I'm ready."

Stanley held the sheath on his belt, feeling somewhat hollow that this man he had hated for five years would die so easily. Nothing would bring Sam back, but no punishment at all would be even more unforgivable.

He drove the knife into Karl's chest and held it there while he stared into Karl's eyes.

"I'm taking you with me to Mallory Keep," Stanley said as Karl struggled to breathe. "I've got a cart out front, waiting for you. Every morning, when I wake up, until your bones turn to dust, I'm going to drive my knife into you once more. You say what happened to Sam was over in seconds? What I have planned for you will take weeks. Maybe months. I'm going to look into your decaying, putrid eyes, and I'm going to remember this moment. And I hope you remember this day and every morning after this while you're burning in the afterlife, you son of a bitch!"

Karl choked on a laugh. He mouthed some choice words that he couldn't give voice to. He patted the loose floorboard once more, and then the light left his eyes. He coughed and laughed no more.

Stanley wiped the knife on Karl's clothes and re-sheathed it. He walked out of the shed and into the light, feeling somewhat lighter. He sent a silent prayer into the sky for Sam.

"Murphy!" he called.

The lieutenant casually walked onto the porch. He put his fingers through his belt loops and raised his eyebrows, waiting for a command.

"Bring the cart around," Stanley said. "I have some garbage that needs picked up."

Murphy nodded and retreated into the house.

Stanley returned to the shed, removed the floorboard and found a medium-sized burlap sack lightly covered in dirt. He untied the simple knot and removed the silver device, which was about the size of a child's torso. Ancient scripts were embedded into its exterior, but these were hard to read, even if he'd known how. Time and the elements had not been kind to it outside of its frozen prison in Xhonia. He remembered digging it out with picks and chisels. It had shown like a beacon through the ice and dirt.

They said it might be 500 years old.

The donkey-pulled cart creaked along the side of the house. The bandit driver rode through the clothesline, driving the clean laundry into the dirt, mud and blood.

"Load him in," Stanley commanded.

"Why save this one?" the driver asked.

"I needed a souvenir."

THE KING RESPONDS

KING AETHIS ELDENWALD sat on an unusually uncomfortable pillow. The halls echoed more than normal, and he was annoyed by every little thing in the throne room. He noticed the remnants of mold in the binding of the stones in the walls. The mannerisms, eccentricities and tics of the nobles below him irritated him. The ambassador in gold from Scythica appeared to smirk at him from the foreign visitors section of the room. He wondered if these armies in his southern territories might be retribution for the murder of their monarch. Perhaps the Visanth Empire had fomented a rebellion within his own houses in retribution.

The torches flickered and flittered as a breeze rolled in from a nearby balcony. The thought of the dead city of Ul Tyrion reminded him that this infighting was not to be taken lightly. Any internal matter could open oneself up to external enemies, just as the dark elves were rumored to have been betrayed. Any weakness in a nation's armor emboldened its enemies and allowed the shadows to creep in and assail it.

Aethis leaned forward on his throne as his spymaster Theodore Crowe ascended the marble steps. Mr. Crowe had just arrived back in the capital from his investigations into the necromancer in the south. He had not yet cleaned up. Aethis had ordered the guards bring him up to the throne room immediately. Mr. Crowe was dressed in a simple brown tunic and cloak and an unshaven face. He did not stop at an acceptable distance, as other guests might. He proceeded all the way up the stairs to the chair itself, bending down to the King's ear so that not even his wife Shea could hear him.

"It's a worst case scenario," Theodore said.

"You're going to have to be more specific," the King said.

"The bandit army has sacked the towns of Perketh and Corinth. When I left, they were heading towards Dona. Mallory has not left his Keep. Dona will fall."

"This is a nightmare," Aethis said. "Our southern lands have withstood orcish invasions for a thousand years, but a single bandit army will bring us to our knees?"

"You didn't send me to scout a bandit army," Theodore said. "I can't say much about them. You told me to find out more about this necromancer."

"He's real?" Aethis asked.

Theodore nodded. "He follows the Red Army. They say he resurrected the entire town of Perketh. The rumors are probably true. His army is large. I'd say he's raised 750 or so undead."

"Are they working together? The bandits and this necromancer?"

"I don't think so," Theodore said. "The Red Army pillages

and kills, and he follows behind them and resurrects their dead. He curses the Red Army for what it did to Perketh. I think the dark elves were right. He's from there."

"What was his army like?"

"Silent," Theodore said. "Unpleasant. He and his people are out for blood. When they find a bandit, they do not simply kill the poor soul. They consume him. I've watched his army eat people in the streets."

Aethis swiveled in his chair, looking along the walls for Godfrey Ross. His general's gleaming armor was nowhere to be found.

"It's time for us to act," the King said. "Where is Godfrey?"

Theodore shrugged. "I just got here, Your Highness. I've been out in the field all week."

His venerable adviser Jurgen Drodd leaned in. "Lord Ross still mourns for his son in the morgue. We have brought him food and water, but he doesn't eat. He rarely speaks."

"It's been a week," Aethis said.

"I fear he may need another," Jurgen replied, withdrawing from the conversation between the spymaster and King Aethis. "He's ordered his son be placed in the ice rooms far below the castle."

"For what possible purpose?" Aethis asked.

"I think he believes it preserves his son's visage," Jurgen said, "so he might visit with him more before he has to bury him."

"Magnus," the King commanded loudly and beckoned him over with his hand.

His eldest son strode forward, bedecked in his purple family colors and white furs.

"The southern lands need your help once more," Aethis

said. "Take two legions, defeat the Red Army, and bring down this necromancer."

Magnus nodded deeply.

"Ragnar will be your second-in-command. Make our family proud!"

"How do you want this necromancer brought to you?" Magnus asked.

"Dead," Aethis said. "Necromancy is forbidden. Burn his body. Bring me his bones."

"Might I advise caution," Theodore said with a small hint of sarcasm. "He is surrounded by an army of the undead."

"Then destroy his men," Aethis said.

"But how do we kill that which is already dead?" his son Ragnar asked.

"Perhaps we should ask the dark elves for guidance," Jurgen advised. "According to the few histories we do have of their people, they have dealt with this kind of magic before."

Aethis nodded at the sound advice. He turned in his chair toward Lord Valedar, the ambassador for Etyria—the kingdom of the dark elves. The ambassador wore his crimson colors and matching cloak. He knelt as his bright green eyes met those of Aethis.

"A necromancer has emerged in the South," Aethis said loudly.

"So you believe us now?" Valedar asked. "The woman was not the culprit?"

"The rumors were true," Aethis said. "How do we kill him?"

The soft-skinned dark elf adjusted his cloak, apparently to give his hands something to do and allow his mind some time to ponder over the request.

"I'm not sure I would advise killing this man," Valedar said.

Magnus scoffed. "You think we should allow a necromancer to walk amongst our lands unopposed?"

"We haven't seen a human necromancer in thousands of years," Valedar said, standing straight. "In each of the fallen cities, we've battled demons and undead. Our enemy uses them. Great King, this may be precisely the type of man we've been looking for. This is the stuff of prophecy."

"Prophecy?" Aethis asked. "What prophecy?"

"Forgive me," Valedar said evasively, "but I'm no oracle. I do not follow prophecies. Many dark elves do. Ever since we first began our fight with the demon hordes, my people have latched onto any small hope we can find. The libraries of Ul Tyrion were once filled with such scrolls, but we are very wary of prophecies at this late hour. Ever since the betrayal at Xhonia—"

"This is the second time you've brought up the paladins in my presence," Aethis said. "How many times must we speak of this?"

"I speak of the Holy One only because it's relevant," Valedar said. "For your kind, Xhonia is ancient history, but for the dark elves? Every child in our city knows what happened five hundred years ago. The paladins revealed themselves to be sworn not to our cause but that of the Holy One. While we battled demons in the caverns below the city, the paladins turned on us as we fought beside them. It was only through catastrophic loss and valiant efforts that we sealed that city in ice."

"And we dissolved the paladin order," Aethis said. "What more do you want from us?"

"We never asked for your ancestor Jalak the Wise to break the paladins over his knee," Valedar said. "We asked for what we have always begged the humans for: aid against the demons. The hordes are coming for us. The three demon lords of the underworld quibble amongst each other, and that is the only thing that has truly stopped them from conquering Uxmal. With Xhonia closed, the hordes continued elsewhere. North then east. Uxmal is all that remains."

"And what does that have to do with the necromancer?"

"If he is one of us," Valedar said, gesturing toward the window and the lands outside. "If he is not tainted by the demons and the Holy One, then perhaps there are other magicians like him who dwell in this land who might help us."

"So, you don't need this necromancer specifically then," Aethis said. "Perhaps you could advise us how to deal with him."

"I beg you to capture him instead of kill him," Valedar said. "Let him tell you his intentions. Perhaps they are not as dark as you imagine."

"He raises the dead," Aethis said.

"I have heard rumors," Valedar said, "that he pursues a bandit army that killed the very people he is raising. I hear his undead kill these wayward men. You asked for my advice, and it is this: ask him to come here and see what powers he possesses. He may be able to aid my people."

"And if he doesn't come willingly?" Aethis asked. "If he attacks my armies?"

"Then cut him down," Valedar said. "Burn him. If he's just a man, he will die."

"And what of his undead?"

"Our experience with the demons has been that when a master dies," Valedar said, "the host falters and splinters. Some fall to the ground and return to the underworld. Some become confused and wander. But all of that may only be true for demon necromancers. I have no experience with human necromancers."

"Why would human necromancers be different?" Jurgen asked.

"I'm no necromancer expert," Valedar said, "and our scholarly works on the subject were lost at Ul Tyrion. All I know is that the demons bind the undead to them. They serve as slaves. None want to be there. If this human does not bind, if he simply leads, the undead may not disperse. I don't know."

"Then who does?" Aethis demanded.

"With your leave," Valedar said, "I can return to Uxmal and search for the answers you seek. My queen or her council may know more about the old works. Or perhaps Oracle Ilsover."

"Very well," Aethis said, rubbing his chin.

The dark elf bowed. He held his pose, and Aethis knew he waited for the King's permission to leave the hall. Aethis waved his hand, and Valedar spun on his heels and briskly stepped from the room.

"The dark elves are no help," Aethis whispered to Theodore and Jurgen.

"The dark elves claim they are under siege," Jurgen said. "Be patient with them."

"And yet," Theodore said, "we're the ones with an army encircling one of our keeps."

Jurgen nodded but raised a finger, speaking as a lecturer might to his class. "The dark elves claim they've been fighting demons from the underworld for thousands of years. Their cities have been shuttered, filled with some cold magic that keeps the darkness at bay. Do you blame them for not coming to our aid immediately with armies when we have never sent our own to stop this phantom demon menace, real or not?"

"After the betrayal of the paladins," Aethis said, "they probably wouldn't have let us into their cities anyway."

"And who could blame them?" Theodore asked.

"What do you want me to do, Father?" Prince Magnus asked.

"Find the Captain of the Guard," Aethis said. "Force him out of his mourning. I need his courage and leadership on the battlefield. Give him drink if you have to. We need men out there who will look death in the face and not flinch."

"I volunteer to accompany your sons," a strong voice hailed from the wall of nobles below. Aethis did not immediately recognize the voice, but he did see familiar features in the man's face as he stepped forward. "Allow me to aid in vengeance on those who caused the death of my friend Frederick Ross."

Aethis knew who this man was. He had seen him in tournaments and knew him as the Lord General's son's best friend.

"Go with my sons, young Lord Jeremy Vossen," Aethis said, "and bring me this necromancer."

"Yes, Your Grace!" Jeremy Vossen vowed.

"Dead?" Magnus asked. "You still want the necromancer dead?"

"Dead or alive doesn't matter to me," Aethis said. "Just stop the madness in the south."

"Alive would be more preferable," Jurgen said. "The dark elves have requested as much. This may be the opportunity we've been looking for to reinforce our relationship."

"Alive then," Aethis said. "Have him delivered to the dark elves at Uxmal."

"My King," Jurgen said, "Might it be better to bring him here first? There are delicate matters of state to discuss with him. We need to ply him for information about his masters and craft before we pass him to the elves. Who taught him? Why is he here? Is he allied with the orcish armies to the south?"

"Very well," Aethis said. "Have him brought here. We'll hand him to the dark elves after Theodore has extracted the information that Jurgen needs."

"Very wise, My King," Jurgen said.

"And the army of undead that surround him?" Magnus asked. "I don't expect them to give up their necromancer lightly. What would you have me do with them?"

"Trample them with cavalry," Aethis said. "Cut their bones from their tendons. Slice them up until they pose no more threat to anyone in my realm, and then take their necromancer. Let them rot in the fields below Mallory Keep or burn them into cinders. General Godfrey will know what to do."

"And the Red Army?" Magnus asked.

"Yes, yes," Aethis said. "The Red Army. I expect it will take your cavalry five days to reach Mallory Keep. Theodore tells me the army of undead is right on the Red Army's tail..."

"The undead march slowly," Theodore said. "They're close, but they stop constantly to raise more corpses. The Red Army is even slower. They pillage, rape and plunder every house and shed they come across. The bandits were entering Dona when I came back to report. The people had time to prepare, and most of the town scattered before the Red Army arrived. Still, I expect the bandit army will not arrive at Mallory Keep for another two days. There are too many houses to check for plunder."

"And you expect the Red Army is no more than five hundred?" Aethis asked.

Theodore nodded. "And skittish as a mouse. The first sight of cavalry and they'll bolt for the forest. This is not an army. It's a loose organization of mayhem and madness."

"Imagine what they'll do when they see the undead," Jurgen said.

"Imagine what any of us would do," Aethis said. He embraced his son Magnus. "But you will not falter. You will charge into their ranks, and you will bring me back this necromancer. You will keep riding until every last bandit in the Red Army is dead or jailed. Leave a legion in the south until no man with a red sash remains."

"Yes, Father."

"Ragnar," Aethis commanded. "Keep your brother safe."

"Yes, Father," Ragnar said.

Aethis nodded once and watched his two sons descend the stairs. He adjourned to his antechamber with Advisor Jurgen and Theodore Crowe. They talked through the night about elves and necromancers, magic and undead, histories and prophecies. His wife checked on him once to make sure he had eaten dinner. She didn't chide him for sending Magnus and Ragnar against the army of the undead, even though he knew it must have been on her mind. He could have sent someone else, but who else could he trust to stand against an army of ghouls?

His general was no coward, but he had suffered a devastating loss. The realm too had lost much promise with the passing of his talented son Frederick. The only other combat veteran in the room had been the young Lord Vossen, who seemed eager enough when the undead were hundreds of miles away.

No, it had to be Magnus.

There was no one else Aethis trusted more to stand his ground and fight the unknown, and Magnus would have his strong brother Ragnar to make sure he came back whole. Shea would forgive him when Magnus returned safe and heralded by the people once more. She would see the wisdom in what had to be done. Eventually.

THE FIRST SKIRMISHES

I N PERKETH, ASHTON had seen death, but in Dona, he had smelled it. A sweet foulness permeated everything here, punctuated by the savory scent of burning flesh somewhere off in the distance. If he were to close his eyes and imagine himself somewhere else, he might not have had such a compulsion to vomit again. But he knew exactly where he was, and the screams of the maimed and the violated made any wayward thought snap right back to the present and the damned.

The reanimated victims of the Red Army followed Ashton as he wandered along the dirt paths and the few cobblestone roadways in the old town. The dead were piled in the streets, waiting for burial carts. Corpses in the poorer sections were more haphazardly scattered, likely laying where their killers had struck them. With each new body, the undead implored him to resurrect. Not with screams like the living in Dona still begging for help. With stares and silence. They hovered near him until he did the only job he seemed qualified for anymore. He felt he lived in a nightmare that he would never wake from.

He thought of the underworld, a dark repository in the center of the world for souls such as these and his own. There was a time when that place scared him more than any other. Eternal life spent in darkness. He knew better now. Damnation was not a quiet, dark hole. Damnation was a life spent amongst the leftovers of the Red Army and the stripping of his humanity. He began to believe that vengeance could not possibly be worth the state his people were in.

He hovered above a small blonde child whose throat had been cut and wondered if he should bring her back. Her holey clothes were in tanned tatters. Blood pooled underneath her neck and her legs, and he dared not lift her tiny shirt to see the extent of her other injuries. Was there any further cause for her to suffer? Did he wish to see her dead, glossy eyes staring back at him, thirsting for vengeance and human flesh? Did he damn each of the victims behind him with a new dark repository in plain sight, here amongst the daylight that served each of them with reminders of the wounds to their chests, necks, faces, and limbs?

Whatever the undead state was, whatever its purpose, he did not want that cruel work to be hers. He closed her eyes, and then he closed his own.

"Dear God," he said, "or Holy One or Creator or whoever is listening. Accept this child into your bosom. Allow no further harm to come to her. Have pity on one of your children. Just one…"

He looked up at the bright sun and pulled his hood up to cover his face, allowing his eyes to retreat into the shadows.

He wasn't trying to hide his tears. The light just seemed almost mocking. The Red Army had cast a long shadow on Dona. No matter how much sunshine bathed the fields and flowers, this was a lightless place indeed.

He laid his hands on the grown men and women. He could feel their presence still. He understood what it meant now. They waited for something to happen. Their souls suffered from shock, hanging over their mangled remains. He imagined the deceased staring down at themselves with unblinking eyes, disbelief etched on ghoulish, otherworldly faces. In Perketh, he had pleaded for them to return. He didn't know what to say. As he raised dozens, his pleas became shorter. By the time he reached Dona, he only used one word.

"Vengeance."

A dark-haired man with a sliced cheek and dislocated shoulder turned his head toward Ashton. They both nodded to each other. There was no more reason to talk. The one word would do. The dead knew why they had been raised, and they needed no instruction on what to do if they encountered a red sash.

Ashton never saw the dead dispatch a Red Army man while he was in Dona, but he knew it was going on. Every once in awhile, he found a red sash with the remnants of entrails and a crimson patch that had freshly soaked the dirt. He knew what the bloody mess was. He had seen them before in the forest a day or two after his friend Clayton had finished eating.

A handful of bandits must have left the main army to pillage and loot Dona. Their greed and gluttony had been their downfall, and the undead of Perketh and the southern lands had visited great retribution upon them. It gave Ashton some comfort to think that a portion of the screams he had heard earlier, the ones that prevented him from imagining himself elsewhere, might have belonged to a dying Red Army man rather than some poor farmer or carpenter in training in Dona.

He crouched over another such bloody patch where a common man lay dead but undisturbed not even ten paces away. This stain had been a Red Army bandit. He looked around at the silent army that marched onward to Mallory Keep, but they averted their eyes from him. Even Clayton, always nearby, seemed embarrassed by the aftermath of their feeding frenzy. Ashton wondered if the undead thought he judged them for eating the bandit, but he did not. He only wanted the deaths to mean something—that this undead retribution would burn a hole in the history of the southern lands that prevented another Red Army from ever happening again.

A woman in a light blue and white dress in the crowd of undead met his gaze, and he smiled at her. Her hair was black and the irises of her glossy eyes matched her dress. She reminded him of Clayton's wife. She smiled back but quickly covered her mouth and ran her fingers through her hair to try to make herself more presentable. It was unnecessary though. Wherever her wounds were, they were not to her face.

In all the time he had led these people from Perketh, he had not tried talking to them. Every time Clayton tried to talk, the wounds to his jaw made his speech garbled. Ashton knew that such failed attempts at simple acts embarrassed his friend, so he only asked rhetorical questions or ones that could be answered with a simple yes or no. Still, days of marching amongst the silent, angry undead made for lonely company. He wondered if she, with her seemingly unblemished face and vocal chords, might talk with him for a while and relieve him of some melancholy.

"What are you doing?" he asked her, pointing to the unnecessary maintenance she had been doing to her hair and face.

"I'm…" the woman said, "sure I look ghastly. I… didn't mean to stare."

"It's a welcome change," he replied. "Many of the people…" He motioned to the throng of undead around her. "They won't look at me here, as I stand near…" He pointed at the blood patch and remnants of tendons and entrails of a bandit.

She nodded solemnly and moved forward, holding her stomach where a wound still leaked blood. "We are changed… but still the same. Our hunger is powerful… hard to stop."

"You can't help yourself," he agreed. He put his hand on Clayton's leg and looked up at him reassuringly and approvingly. "You must eat, just as I do."

He looked back at the recently deceased middle-aged man who lay next to the remains of the bandit. "Yet, you do resist the urge."

"The urge is strong," she said, "but the need for vengeance is stronger. This man may help you. He may help us. No one wanted the bandit to return. He was an evil man."

"So," he said. "You ate the bandit to prevent him from being resurrected?"

"No, no!" she cried. "I haven't eaten anyone. I… You only raised me a couple days ago. This was done by the older ones. I simply watch. I wait…"

"You wait for what?"

She looked toward the southeast, the direction that the bandit army had moved toward. "I will only eat one man—

the one who violated me and my family. The one who stabbed me in the stomach and pulled the knife upward."

She closed her eyes and covered her wounds.

"Do not be embarrassed of your wounds," he said. He stood up and spoke louder for all who followed near him. "Your wounds are not marks of shame. They are reminders of what we still must do. I thank you for not consuming the innocent. I know now that you have shown amazing restraint. Now, show courage. Do not be afraid that the living might abhor, fear or loathe you."

The undead looked at him and gathered around. He walked to a nearby porch, likely the home of the man who had been murdered on the street. Once Ashton was behind the shoddy banister, he addressed the crowd once more.

"Instead, be proud that you have come back. Be strong and support each other. Hold your heads up high and walk together with purpose."

He nodded as the crowd nodded, but inwardly, he was worried. He had no idea where he was going or even what he was doing. He only knew that he must keep going forward.

"I have no great strategies," he admitted to them. "I know nothing of battles or cavalries or archery. It's true that I have made armor and arrows, but I had more to do with the makings of cups and silverware. And yet, here I am with you, and we've come this far."

Something like a cheer came back at him from the undead. It was tempered somewhat by injuries, and there were more wheezes and coughs than intelligible words, but there was enthusiasm in their cries. Their eyes were furious and rapturous.

"Some of you have called me Master," he said. "I do not

see myself as such. I know not the rules or laws that bind you to me. I don't know how long you are here. All I know is that as long as you are here, I will be beside you. We will find this Red Army."

Another cheer.

"We will chase them out of our towns and into the forests!" he promised.

A louder cheer as more undead pushed into the crowd around the porch.

"And as they stumble, you will be upon them," he said. "This hunger you feel is no doubt the divine retribution that the gods of our world have demanded. For it is not me who resurrected you. I cannot believe that. I am no scholar of magic or the occult. I have no wisdom to teach others and multiply this strange craft. All I know is that I have stood over you, and I have asked you to come back. It was you, not I, who clawed your way back into the world of the living! I am but a man who walks alongside you, not a Master!"

He found the undead raven-haired woman in the blue dress. He smiled at her, remembering her answers to his questions. She grinned back. Her demeanor seemed to have changed though. She listened intently and no longer favored her wound.

"I have asked you to take vengeance on the men of the Red Army," he continued. "I have asked you to avenge yourselves on those who have wronged and killed you and taken your families. Look not to me for your redemption. I am not the instrument of your retribution. You are! Only you can stop this army, and every step we fall behind, they take more children from their mothers. More husbands from their wives.

"Do not linger here in Dona with me. My work here is slow, and I feel that keeping you here is only causing you more pain and keeping you away from your final, deserved rest. I am of no more use to you there than I am here. I seek only to ask more here to join you—to accompany you to wherever this chase may end. Do not look to me for orders. You know in your heart what you must do. Bring your anger to them, wherever they have gone."

Despite his words, the crowd continued to look to him for guidance. He grew frustrated. He put his hands on the banister and begged them to listen.

"The Red Army is to the southeast," he shouted, "and yet you are here with me, walking amongst the undead, the destitute and the lost. Do not linger here. Go! Find the Red Army. Go now, and do not stop until every last one of them is dead."

After a few moments of confused looks, the crowd dispersed and poured around the house. He watched them jostle against each other like a tightly-packed flock of birds. Dozens and then hundreds stomped along the dirt and the cobblestones until the boards rattled against the rickety house.

He turned around and found the woman in the blue dress still standing there. She was the only undead person not moved to stampede with the mob. She smiled at him queerly.

"I take it my words had no effect on you," he said as he approached the man he had been standing over.

"I wouldn't say that," she said. "Just different. To them, you are a master. To me, you are a curiosity."

He processed her words and looked at her as he approached another dead man.

"What do you find curious about me?" he asked.

"You remind me of someone," she said.

"Who's that?"

"A great general of the durun," she said. "He loved his

people very much. He died serving them. Ultimately, he failed the durun, but he tried."

Perhaps, Ashton was wrong. He wasn't sure he wanted to continue conversing with the undead. Perhaps it was better to have more with mouth injuries like his friend Clayton. Ashton smiled politely, and stooped over the man he had noticed a moment ago. His spirit was strong, hovering there above the body and beside the remains of the bandit.

A door creaked behind him, just past the porch he had made his speech from.

"Are you the Necromancer?" a young girl asked.

"No one has called me such to my face," he said, "but if there was a man more qualified to answer to the title, then I don't know him."

The young girl, no more than five years old, opened the door and slipped through. She shyly and clumsily made her way down the stairs, and fidgeted at the remains of her filthy shirt and long, dirty dress. She had blonde hair, similar to his own, and he felt immediately sorry for her.

"Are you going to raise Daddy?"

"Would that be ok?" he asked.

She nodded vigorously. "He… he…" She struggled to form a coherent sentence, as most five year olds often do. "I need him here! He's supposed to… He needs to take me to school and go to the market and…"

"The market's on fire," Ashton said, profoundly aware that this young girl had not grasped the magnitude of the destruction of Dona and that life as she had known it was over. "Your school is probably gone too. Your teacher at the school, if she is still alive, may not come back."

"But I liked..." the girl said. "I loved her stories... the old gods... the wood elves! Those were my favorite!"

"Those were your favorite?" he asked, trying to force a smile, despite the death and destruction around him. Not even a hundred yards away, one of her neighbor's homes was still smoldering. Charred bodies were visible in the yard.

"The elves spend all their time hanging from trees," she said, excited but distracted with her fidgeting at what cloth still clung to her body. "If we had a tree, I'd hang from it. Daddy planted one in the back for my last birthday, but it's too small to hang from."

"It'll grow," Ashton said.

"But Daddy said he would make me a swing. I tried to wake him... but... he won't get up. Maybe you can wake him?"

Ashton looked over the man and then back up at the woman in the blue dress. She raised her eyebrows at him to indicate that she was merely here to observe.

"I am the Necromancer," he said, "and I can feel your father here with us. I believe I can give him back to you."

The girl stomped her feet and jumped up and down at the foot of the stairs to her home.

"Don't get too excited," he warned. "You've seen the ones around me. All of the men and women who followed me here from Perketh..."

The girl nodded.

"Your father would be like these people."

The girl cast her eyes downward and held her hands at her stomach. "Would he eat me?"

"Would he eat you?" Ashton asked, confused and appalled.

"I watched them from the window," the girl said, "when they ate that bad man. They were like wild dogs. Daddy told me to stay away from wild dogs because they eat people. I can only go after them if I have a big stick, and only if there's one of them, never two. That's what Daddy says. Says when they're a pack, they get madder, and a stick won't be enough to scare them off. If Daddy turns into a wild dog, I don't think he'll be scared of a stick, even if he's not with the others."

Ashton looked at her with horror, at the rationalization of her own father becoming a wild thing if he came back. He had never really thought of the undead that way—there really hadn't been enough time to consider what he had done in bringing people back as cannibals.

"I don't know much," Ashton said, "but I don't think your dad would come back as a wild dog. When I brought my best friend Clayton back, he remembered me. He followed me and made sure no harm came to me. He has protected me, like your Daddy did to the dogs."

"Then bring him back," she demanded shyly. "With all the people and trash in the streets, the dogs will come back. He's better at scaring them off. And he promised me a swing…"

Ashton's eyes watered as he looked at her. He placed a hand on her father's shoulder, but his gaze never left the young girl.

"What's your name?" he asked her.

"Margie," she replied.

"Short for Margaret?"

She nodded.

"My mother's name was Margaret," he said. "And what's your father's name?"

"Albert."

"That's a good name," he said.

"He's a good Daddy."

"Albert," Ashton said, finally looking down at the man and speaking firmly. "Your daughter needs you. Return to her."

Albert's eyes opened, and he looked first at Ashton and then at Margie. Albert smiled and cried as he stumbled to his feet.

"Honey," he said, grasping his side where a sword or dagger had ended his life. "Margie, are you ok?"

"I'm fine," she said as she put her arm around him.

Albert put his arm around her and ascended the stairs back to his home. He turned around as he reached the door, and Ashton noticed the father had left a streak of blood on his daughter's dirty shirt.

"Thank you," Albert said simply.

"Make the most of whatever time you have," Ashton said. "I don't know how long this magic will last."

Albert nodded before opening the unlocked door and pulling his daughter inside the house.

The woman in blue continued to smile queerly at him.

"So this general you were talking about?" he asked her.

"General Maddox," the woman said.

"Who did he lead again?"

"The durun," she said.

"Never heard of them," Ashton said.

"They are what I am," she said.

"And who are you?" he asked.

"I have many names," she said. "Some terrible. Some quite flattering. But who I am is unimportant right now. Who are you?"

"I didn't actually raise you, did I?" he asked, standing up and dusting his palms against each other.

"Not in the way you think, no. You know that all these people will die, right?"

"Ma'am," Ashton said. "These people have already died."

She chuckled. "What is your name?"

He could have answered her, but he felt a compulsion to defy her request. He did not know why, but he felt the conversation had taken on an importance—that he could not dismiss it flippantly. There had to be a reason that this undead woman was talking to him when no one else had. Besides, she claimed she was not undead. She was something else. Why had she approached him as someone he had resurrected?

"I asked yours first," he said, "and you didn't answer. Why should I?"

"It's not a simple thing for me," she said, her blue eyes appearing to grow darker in hue. Her features became more accentuated. Her bosom plumped. Her hips grew wider. She cocked her head. "I'm not from here. Neither are my people. Names do not mean the same thing where I come from, and the way you pronounce them is quite different. I've come a long way to find something. Now, I wonder if I'm here to find *someone* too."

"Are you an elf?"

She laughed with a sweet richness. He found himself moving toward her.

Her dress grew darker. Then black. Whatever wounds had been there on her stomach disappeared. Her lips grew redder. She exuded a type of sexuality that was dangerous and alluring.

"For a long time," she said, "there were those among my kind, the durun, who called me Queen. Like so many young people, I let the titles get to my head. I thought I would rule the universe. That's where General Maddox failed his people. I have put men against men and dark beings against dark beings since before this world even took shape out of the celestial mists. My titles are ancient. My names are infinite."

"Are you a goddess?" he asked.

She smiled and placed a finger on his lips. "Careful," she said. "I'm very susceptible to flattery, and I sense in you a large void in what I consider my specialty. Be very careful what you say to me, young mortal. I might make you my pet, and my pets never last. For now, I'm an admirer. Let's leave it at that."

"Then what should I call you?"

She groaned slightly. "What do you want?"

"I want what's right by my people," Ashton said. "I want to right the wrongs of this world."

She laughed heartily. "Oh, you sweet, sweet thing. So pure. Can it be true? Here? So close to where the Vision of Maddox rests? How far do you hope to go? What would you do for your people?"

Her fingers walked up his arm, and her nails had grown long and impressive. Her once blue dress had split from the top, revealing overwhelming cleavage that was covered only thanks to the flimsiest of two clasps. He felt an urge to undo them. His eyes drifted to her now exposed belly button, and as he looked down, her dress seemed to retreat and grow tighter. Her clothing seemed almost pasted on now. The cloth grew darker and darker until it was black as night.

"There are men who worship me," she said. "Men who cry out in the night for the power to smite those who cross the boundary to this world through the old cities, where the elves failed to keep the bad men at bay. And I have given them that power, at some small cost. What power do you seek so that I might shower you with it?"

"What should I call you?" he asked again as her hands and fingernails roamed around his shoulders.

"What do you crave?" she purred. "For my name depends on your desires."

"What do the men who cry out in the night for power call you?"

"Which men?" she asked. "For there are many."

Ashton sensed that he was in danger, but he found it extremely difficult to stop looking at her and break away. She had a magnetism about her, and not just because of the overt and powerful sexuality that she exuded. There was something very unnatural about her. Even supernatural.

"The durun lords called me Queen," she said, "and they sought me out. I do appreciate those who call me Queen. I created the naurun and brought forth many of their greatest lords. I've created many things, even on this world. I'm a champion of nature. I was the first to look past the Abyss and discover life outside of our shadows."

"What are the naurun?"

"You might call them demons…"

"Demons?" Ashton asked. "You created demons?"

"Experiments that got out of hand," she said. "Some of my creations have been quite tame, in comparison. Look, I'm a leap-first kind of lady. If I see something I want to pounce on, I just…"

She let the thought trail as her fingernail scraped through the brown cloth on his shoulder.

"So, demons are real?" Ashton asked, breaking away from her touch.

"Have you not seen them?" she asked. "I've been fighting them for ten thousand years in your plane alone. It's exhausting, really. And to think the humans above the battle think nothing of our toils…"

She exaggerated a sigh and cast him a sultry look. "I could use a leader like you. A new Maddox. Someone who inspires like you do. Someone who wouldn't be lured into a trap set by demons. Someone with your passion…"

"You want me to fight demons?"

"Is there any other battle worth fighting?" she asked. "Why stay up here and get yourself involved in petty bickering between bloated lords? What happens when the Red Army lies under your boot? Where then will you send your army of undead?"

"Where will I send them?" Ashton asked. "I would release them. Their vengeance would be done. I'd allow them to return to the underworld."

She stopped groping at him. "How boring…"

"You may have some larger purpose," he said. "You may be some dark goddess…"

She groaned again and grinned mischievously at him. "I have told you to be careful with your compliments…"

"But I am just a man," Ashton continued. "If I had some larger purpose, it dies with the Red Army. That's my purpose now. I'm not this general that you seek."

"You may have been born a man," she said, "just as the Prince of Demons was born a lowly naurun. But I raised him up to be something else entirely. Now, demons tremble at his name, and he trembles at mine."

She laughed luxuriously and richly. "Though, he trembles after me much differently than his hordes do for him."

"And what name does he tremble to?" Ashton asked.

"Who does he fear, you mean?" she asked.

"Does he fear you? Or adore you?"

She smirked and laughed again. "Perhaps one day you may ask him. See if he knows the difference."

"You still haven't answered my question," Ashton said.

"Which one?"

"The same one I've repeated over and over again."

"Ask it again."

He thought he might try flattering her.

"What should I call you, dark goddess?"

She smiled genuinely. "That'll do."

"But what does this Prince of Demons call you?"

She gritted her teeth. "For a man who claims he's just a man, you surely are adept at maneuvering me into corners without giving me what I want. That's not to say I dislike a good dark corner. I've pulled my share of creatures into such places when the desire has struck me. But I can see in your eyes that your corner has no such delightful intents. Fair enough. I'll answer your question. The naurun who calls himself the Prince of Demons calls me Mekadesh, when he wishes to find me in his bed. It's a bit of a joke between us."

"Is that the name you would have me call you?"

"No," she admitted. She circled him, eyeing him like a fox might watch a hen. "I do not intend to mislead you. I believe I have use for you."

She was intoxicating, in a way. He wanted to watch her too, but there was a stronger part inside him that told him to resist. No woman had ever talked to him or looked at him like this, and she admitted to having an ulterior motive. Giving in to her simply fed that motive, whatever it was.

"If I am to be of use to you," he said, "then I will have to know your name."

Her lip snarled ever so slightly, but her aggravation melted away quickly. Her words began to melt over him like honey once more. "You wish to know my name so that you might call to me?"

She ran her fingers up his chest, and despite his thick cloak and doublet, it felt like her fingernails were on his bare body. He felt goosebumps form across the entirety of his skin, from neck to toe.

His eyes followed her hands as they moved downward, but his mind jolted at the sight of the gore left by his ghouls on the ground behind her. He saw other bodies far away, down the streets. Whatever effect she might have tried to have was weakened by the state of Dona. His eyes wandered.

"I wish only to call to the dead and the damned," he said. "These are my people."

"The dead can wait," she said. "They have all the time in the world."

He felt their presence. He couldn't see them, but he felt their pull toward bodies lost between his world and the underworld. Spirits hovering over their corpses.

"They call to me," he said.

"Yes," she said, still rubbing on his shirt. He felt frozen in place, despite the pull from down the street toward other ghosts. "And what do they ask for? Who do they call to?"

"You're still trying to coax me out of my name?"

She sighed, playing with his chest hair through the top of his plain tunic. "You do not have to guard this from me. Your name holds no power over you. You're only human."

He felt that she wasn't lying, but he kept her there looking at him. She hadn't breathed for a few moments, not that he knew she needed to breathe. All he knew was that her eyes shimmered in anticipation.

"My parents named me Ashton," he said finally.

Her eyes grew wide and she pulled away from him, smiling triumphantly.

"Jeraldson," she said. "Yes, yes. I know you."

"How do you know me?"

"Son of Karl and Margaret. Both are here with me now in the Underworld."

"My father is dead?"

He said it out of curiosity. There was no initial feeling to it. He had given his father so little thought that the idea that his father might die hadn't even occurred to him. To Ashton, Karl was almost like a cancer. Karl killed others, like his mother, and then just disappeared while normal people were grieving.

She nodded.

"How do you know that?" he asked.

"I told you," she said, "that I have no intention of misleading you. I tell you the truth."

"Then how did he die?"

"He was killed by the Red Army," she said. "Murdered by the man who calls himself The Archer. Stanley Shiloh. You met him once in a forest. Your friend Clayton smashed Stanley's friends to pieces with a rock. Your friend ate them, in point of fact. The Archer is the instigator of the mob. Your counterpart. A transient nemesis. A no one. Not like you at all. You will be more."

Ashton remembered the man who had shot Clayton with three arrows in the forest. The Archer and two others had tried to rob him, but he had nothing. Clayton had fought them off single-handed and chased the bowman into the woods.

"Thank you," he said. "When I think of the Red Army, I'll remember The Archer. It'll give me focus. A target for my rage. A target for my people."

"I've given you some useful information, have I not?" she asked. "Perhaps some form of payment is due."

"I gave you my name," he said, "and you gained information I had not intended. You told me my name meant nothing to me; that I was only human. Was this not misleading? Have you not already violated whatever contract in truth we had been working under?"

"Perhaps," she admitted playfully. "I'm not accustomed to being honest."

She ran her fingers down his chest and lingered at his yarn belt. Through his layers of clothing, he felt her hard nails on his stomach, and she played to this with great effect by pulling on the yarn and moving her fingers slowly along its length from hip to hip. He stirred to her touch.

She giggled.

"I'm here looking for something," she said. "It was lost to me ages ago, back when my people first started calling me Queen. Soon, I will claim it, for it is mine and within reach. You could do the same. I'm in need of a new general—someone who will help me fight demons. I believe it could be you. When you finish with this vendetta of yours, seek me out."

"I still do not know your name," he said again.

"Since you will not voice your desires," she said, "then giving you a name to call me is… difficult to do. To lessen my disappointment, I'll think of this as a prelude to a game between you and me. A sort of introductory period. It's enough for me to know your name, so that I might call on you again."

She released his belt, but the sensation stayed with him

long after she departed. He felt her fingers running along his belt as she waved goodbye at him, and then, without any warning whatsoever, she disappeared. He could still see her naked belly and the dark dress that barely supported her curvy hips and curvaceous body in his mind's eye.

Someone cleared their throat behind him, and he knew who it was by the tone. He had heard a similar mannerism of disappointment from the man for many years.

"Don't judge me," Ashton called to his friend. He fought against his robe to hide the bulge that this mysterious Queen had brought about.

Clayton grunted and waited. Ashton hustled along the path toward his best friend and together they approached another victim of the Red Army. This one was a tanned man with hard callouses on his hands and a deep gash to his abdomen. Ashton felt the man's presence.

"Vengeance," he said simply.

Clayton grunted in appreciation beside him, and within seconds, the man had risen to his feet. Clayton pointed toward the direction of the Red Army's advance, and the nameless man grasped his stomach as he limped along the path out of town. Ashton stepped into the house and found the man's wife in the living room.

"Vengeance."

Another enthusiastic volunteer for his large bandit-seeking posse.

Again and again, Ashton visited the houses and streets of Dona, and each time, the recently deceased joined him before walking or even running down the road to Mallory Keep. He stayed there for nearly a full day, and those living who remained hidden and avoided the plague of bandits brought him small bits of cheese, bread, and even jerky.

In the crowd of revelers and well-wishers were several men in religious habits, including a young monk in thick gray wools who hailed him and smiled.

"Godspeed," the young man said as Ashton mounted a young gray gelding with a simple saddle that wandered the street.

"I don't think the gods have anything to do with this," Ashton admitted. "We unfortunate creatures are unfavored by the gods or even the King. Even our lords, who are sworn to watch over us, trample us with their carriages and allow bandits to murder more of us still."

"The gods are cruel," the monk replied, "or maybe the world is cruel and the gods fight against it in their own way. Even amongst the clergy of the gods, we do not know their designs. Perhaps you are their creature. Perhaps you are the gods' necromancer."

Ashton shook his head.

"Look not to the gods for salvation," he said. "If they really wanted to stop all of this death and heartache, we'd all be immortal—untouched by disease and blight and impervious to sword."

"Perhaps that is not in their power," the monk said. "Perhaps there is no break in the cycle of life and death. All they can do is create someone like yourself and encourage him out into the world and amongst the people. To do right by them."

"Or perhaps I am simply one of the people," Ashton said. "Perhaps I draw my power from all of you, to serve you in these small tasks that will surely be forgotten in the annals of time."

"I assure you this will not be forgotten," the monk said. "You may be right that the gods may forget us in our time of need. I think not, but it is not my place to know the thoughts of gods or even men. But you? You will be remembered. For as you say, you are one of us. A necromancer of the people. I will write your name in the books of my order, in the Halls of Godun."

"What is your name, monk?"

"I am called Thomas," the monk said.

"Well, Thomas," Ashton said. "As you have promised to remember me, I will remember your name. If we should meet again, I will hail you as Thomas of Godun."

"I'll look forward to that," Thomas said. He bowed his head, crossed his hands over his chest and intoned a simple prayer. "May your journey be eventful and your cause ever righteous."

Ashton smirked as Clayton walked alongside his new horse. He waved to the crowd of twenty or so survivors.

"Take care of my husband," a woman called out.

"Make sure my daughter finds her way back to the Underworld!" a man yelled.

"I'll do what I can," Ashton said.

As the horse cantered through the streets, Ashton caught sight of another rider in the far tree line. Cloaked in black. A yellow mark on his chest, like the sun breaking the horizon. He paid the rider no mind. He had heard no tale of the dark knight of the woods helping the people of Dona.

"What use is a paladin anyway?" he muttered to the bloody streets and the desolate faces.

THE SIEGE BEGINS

J
ULIAN MALLORY STOOD atop the highest battlements of Mallory Keep, looking down, far below, at the
men running about in their red sashes. Beside him, a
four-squared black-and-white flag of his house snapped in the
strong winds. The bandit army had formed a makeshift camp
along the main road to the castle, within full view and, likely
unbeknownst to the Red Army, in range of the castle's siege
weapons. Julian counted a dozen common supply wagons,
stolen from the towns and families the outlaws had pillaged
from and murdered.

The Red Army had given the Mallory estate plenty of
warning, and the Keep was well stocked. It had been built to
withstand an orcish army with ballista and catapults, and this
rabble was nothing but men with sticks, bows and torches.
The outer walls were twice as tall as those in the capital and
more than half as thick.

"I need but fifty men to disperse the lot," Julian said, "or we could loose arrows and bolts from the ballistae."

His father grunted.

"We have pigeons from Corinth," Janus said, "that claim there is another larger army in tow. We wait for their appearance. We don't know their intent."

Janus produced a thin piece of white parchment from his robe. Julian was also dressed in nothing but a black-and-white robe, his dark hair flowing down his back. His sister Jayna leaned against his arm, wrapping her own arms around his and bracing against him as the wind whipped around the Mallories.

Julian snatched the paper and read it.

The first army will be at your door in a day. A much larger second army trails behind. We believe they are locals from Perketh, injured but eager.

Julian held the message in front of Jayna. She feigned some interest before burying her head back into his triceps. He handed the missive back to his father, who pocketed it.

Julian leaned against the flagpole on top of the inner wall. He stared down at the killing fields that stretched along the gap between the outer and inner walls. No orcish army had penetrated here in 700 years, and then only because the old keep had been made of wood. After the 50 foot thick and 100 foot tall outer wall had been gifted to them by King Gerald the Builder, Mallory Keep had stood undefeated, despite hundreds of orcish raids and skirmishes with southern lords.

A sergeant rushed through a nearby door, his plate armor clattering noisily.

"What is it, Myers?"

Myers saluted smartly. "A knight has returned from a raiding party we sent out many days ago, Sire."

"And?" Janus asked.

"He says he saw Frederick Ross die," the sergeant said. "He said he wishes to make a full account."

"Later," Janus said. "Tell him to wait downstairs."

"Very well, Milord."

"Shall we go inside for breakfast?" Janus asked, looking to Julian and Jayna as if the news of the death of one of the most famous people in the realm meant nothing.

Julian nodded.

"Myers," Janus said. "I don't want any other interruptions until we're done."

"Yes, Milord," Myers said. He bowed curtly and left back through the door and nearby stairs.

Janus briskly walked to the penthouse atop the wall. Julian pulled himself from his sister's clutches. She groaned in protest, so he rubbed the sides of her arms to warm her before following his father to the parapet door. His father seemed to only think of them as affectionate and his sister as cold-natured. He still did not appear to grasp the truth of Julian and Jayna's relationship.

The breakfast was normal for the Mallory house, each meal individually prepared by the master chef Jormung, a transplant from Kingarth. Jayna enjoyed poached eggs and a side of pork sausage. Julian had his usual duck breast with scrambled eggs and toast. Their father dined on a rare steak, which was his custom before battles. He claimed there was no better preparation for a bloody day.

As they were finishing their main course, Myers entered the penthouse dining room and bowed to Janus.

"I thought I told you not to interrupt us," Janus said.

"Sir," the man in the polished spaulders and chain-mail said, "the second army has arrived. They fight with the Red Army."

"The second army fights the first?" Julian asked.

"Indeed," the sergeant said.

Julian put down his fork and knife and casually walked over to the battlements. He could hear screams and the distant sounds of battle. As he looked down, past the outer wall, he saw only streaks of blood on the field and the blur of men running into the trees. Their pursuers moved more like animal than man, and when they caught up to their prey, gore sprayed into the air in fine mists and entrails.

"What the—?" Julian said.

His father strode briskly to a spot beside him. His sister raised her hand to her mouth at the doorway. Each of them stood transfixed, watching men behaving like orcs.

"It's unconscionable," Julian said. "These are men from Perketh? Our Perketh? I drove through there only—"

He remembered the carriage ride, and the dalliance with Jayna that resulted in a dead local. He didn't turn to look at her, but he knew her eyes were on him. He didn't say another word.

A man in a brown cloak on a gray horse cantered within hailing distance of the wall. Around him, men and women dragged screaming Red Army bandits into the woods. The man did not seem bothered by the slaughter. He continued to push his horse closer to the castle.

"Is this how you protect your people?" the man yelled, his voice just barely reaching them atop the high wall.

Julian and his father looked at each other and then back

down at the speck of a man below. Julian strained to hear the man.

"Are you no longer content with running us down one at a time with your carriages?" the man asked. "Now, you must allow armies to come in and slaughter us at such larger scale?"

Julian gulped.

"Who are you?" Janus called loudly. "Why are you here?"

A woman on the field grew tired of dragging her screaming prey into the forest. She threw his feet to the ground, straddled him, and drove her fists into the man's skull until he cried no more. She didn't stop until the contents of the man's head poured onto the ground and then she began devouring his innards.

"What madness is this?" Janus asked.

"This is the madness you have wrought upon us," the man in the brown cloak stated. "When you allowed these men to slaughter the entire town of Perketh. You waited here... Did you not? And why? For what purpose did you hide behind these walls when that same army sacked and slaughtered Dona? To save yourself? To eat breakfast? Perhaps you were too busy to save us."

The man's horse grew uneasy with the slaughter around it. It paced and neighed, as people were dragged to their deaths nearby. The rider pulled his reins to force the horse to face the castle once more.

"You created this chaos!" the man accused. "Do you now complain about the manner in which your subjects seek their justice? After you have given them no recourse?"

Julian became distracted by a pair of men fighting over the corpse of a man with a red sash near the wagon camp along the roads. They yanked and pulled at him so hard that he split in two. The ghouls raced into the nearby woods with their bloody parcels.

"What is your name, boy?" Janus demanded.

The man did not respond for a long minute. Instead, the horse continued to pace and complain, and the rider corrected the beast.

"Name yourself!" Julian echoed.

"You are the second person to demand my name in as many days," the man said. "What power does this thing give you? Will you send soldiers to my house?"

"I ask only because I'm curious," Janus shouted.

"Why aren't you curious about the names of the people you lost in Perketh and Dona?" the man asked. He pointed to the woman who had bashed a man's head in and was devouring him. "Do you not want to know what her name was before you let her die and forced her to live like this?"

The necromancer pointed at a man who was eating a bandit's shoulder and then at another who was ripping out entrails. He pointed to others nearby in the forest, splashing blood against tall grass, shrubs and trees.

"But maybe you're right," he yelled to them. "Maybe none of their names would have mattered to you."

He sat atop his horse, watching the undead killing and eating for a time.

"Bakers and butchers," the man finally said. "Ironmen and smiths. Housewives and laundry women. Their names mean nothing to them now. They didn't need you to know their names. They needed your protection. Have you no shame?!"

Julian stared at a pair of children who gnawed at the arms of a man who watched their grisly work on his person in shock. The panicked cries had died down. All Julian could hear was the crack of sticks as the forests gave way to the fiends, chasing their quarry through the bushes and the undergrowth that hid the atrocities of the second army.

"Do you come for us?" Lord Janus asked.

"Do you admit you've done wrong?" the man asked, looking up at them through the bright sun. "Do we, the people, have cause for retribution?"

"We did not sack our own towns," Janus said. "We will make things right. The King will be informed and…"

"Make recompense?" The man shouted. "Do you not see? Do you not see what's going on down here?"

He pointed to the scenes of carnage all around him. A young girl with blonde hair ripped a dead man's hair from his scalp. A large woman slowly and methodically head-butted a man's skull into mush. A young boy stabbed a faceless bandit over and over again. A man plunged two fistfuls of guts into his mouth near the abandoned cart caravan.

The rider walked his horse slowly toward the abandoned bandit caravan. He stopped short of the man consuming fistfuls of flesh. The perpetrator of the bloody attack looked up at the rider and appeared to panic. He wiped his hands in the grass, and Julian could hear muffled cries as the horror of the cannibalism dawned on the undead man consuming the flesh.

The rider came down from his horse and comforted the man and looked at the grisly work. The overwhelmed undead man ran into the woods as the rider closed the eyes of the dead man who had been half eaten.

"Are you the one they call the Necromancer?" Janus yelled.

The rider walked into the caravan, closing the eyes of others who had died, some of whom had not been further violated. The members of the second army began to appear from the forest, where no further cries echoed from. The bandits had either successfully escaped or had been overwhelmed and fallen. The commonly-dressed folk were covered in blood.

"These men and women of Perketh and Dona," Janus said, "are they your creatures?"

"They are no one's creatures!" the man replied. "They are free men and women! You released them from your service when you let them die."

"Do they still breathe?"

"You ask me if they are still alive?" the rider asked.

"Speak plainly," Janus said, "or do not speak at all."

The men, women and children along the forest's edge began to walk toward the castle. Many appeared hurt and limped or even dragged their way toward the walls of the keep.

The rider moved through the bandit camp, closing more eyes. If he was the Necromancer, he made no effort to showcase his gifts with these freshly dead men. Perhaps, he thought the bandits had gotten what they deserved.

The rider stopped behind an open carriage and gazed at what must have been another body. He reached into the back of the wooden deck and pulled at a naked creature, eventually bringing it to the ground and slapping its face to try to revive it.

Far below, Julian could hear the sound of hands and fists slamming into the stone outer wall. He looked down to see many of the common folk hammering away at the exterior of Mallory Keep, but these fortifications were rated to withstand direct attacks from siege weapons. Even the strongest of men did nothing but bloody their knuckles.

"Loose a wave of arrows at them," Lord Janus commanded Sergeant Myers.

"Should we aim near them or at them?" Myers asked.

"They attack our walls," Lord Janus said. "We mustn't tolerate such acts, especially from our own subjects. It's time for this mob to disperse. Fill a few of them with arrows. If they persist, loose some pitch and light it."

The Sergeant hurried along the walkway and down a nearby stairwell. His steps echoed until they disappeared, and Julian watched as a line of fifty archers were summoned along one of the parapets.

The men pounding their fists against the lower walls were but a handful of the necromancer's army. At least a thousand men and women still stood in full view along the edge of the forest, possibly waiting for orders from the rider.

"Should I gather the knights?" Julian asked, pointing toward the wood. "We could disperse the men along the forest."

"Let's see how they react first," his father said. "I want to see just how motivated his loyal subjects are."

Julian nodded and looked back to the remains of the main bandit camp. The rider had pulled a naked man from the carriage and hoisted him atop the rider's horse, which he led into the forest.

"It appears our speaker has lost his stomach for battle," Janus said.

Julian nodded again.

He heard the twang of arrows leaving bowstrings and watched as the deadly projectiles descended to the ground. He held his breath as he counted the seconds before impact. Half the arrows found their mark, and Julian watched as the front line of men staggered backward and faltered. Some fell to the ground, but most recovered quickly and looked up at the Mallories.

With grim determination, the dozens of men below returned to their feet and the work of pounding against the wall.

"Remarkable," Julian said.

"Let loose the pitch!" Janus commanded.

A five man crew pushed a seventy gallon vat of boiling pitch until the contents poured down the wall. The nasty liquid clumped and rolled down the slanted walls for several seconds, forming balls of black tar that mowed over some of the men, who did not try to dodge them. Torches fell from the ramparts, and fire spread down the walls inexorably toward the bloodthirsty attackers.

In horror, Julian watched as emblazoned men continued to hammer their fists into the stone walls. None left their task. They only stopped pounding at the impenetrable brick when their bodies collapsed to the earth in a heap of charred bones and ash.

"Should I gather the knights?" Julian asked again.

"And fight these undead with swords?" Janus asked rhetorically. "No, I think not. Let us stay within our walls for a while. Take your sister inside and bring up a scholar from the library. See if there is a precedent in our books. Bring up someone from the Order of Godun, if you can find one. Make sure they see this, and find me some answers."

"Yes, father," Julian said.

Julian looked once more to the forest, where the rider had left the battlefield carrying a dead man on his horse. Three men now followed the necromancer. A dark knight on a white horse approached from the west along the forest edge. A dark-skinned man followed the dark knight from the shadows to the east. A large undead man with the build of a blacksmith limped further behind.

"I would see you go immediately," his father stated, breaking him from his gaze.

Julian turned toward the nearby door where they had emerged from breakfast and prepared to return to his room far below where he needed to change from his robes.

"And son?" Janus called.

Julian turned from the doorway.

"Yes, father?"

"Until this is over," Janus said, "take Jayna to the ground floor and stay near the main tunnels that lead to the southern waterways. Pack everything you might need for a long journey. If anything should happen, if these undead break into this castle, you take your sister and escape together to the south. Take Master Kraytos with you and travel across the Small Sea, if you must. The House of Mallory must not fall. Even to the undead."

Julian faltered. His father was not the type to easily scare. He hadn't even balked at the news that Captain Ross had fallen, despite the fact that the King and the Lord General might end up holding his father accountable. But this undead army appeared to trigger something close to an emotion—a preservation instinct for himself and his sister. He felt his great shame welling inside him. He felt his knees growing weaker, wanting to prostrate himself before his father and begging his forgiveness for falling in love with Jayna.

"Go!" Janus said.

Julian forgot his shame. He nodded quickly and escaped into the dining room, where he tried to process what had just happened. Jayna nestled her arm under his and held his hand as they walked silently toward their rooms. His skin embla-zoned at her touch, and the danger of their situation allayed his fears about the discovery of their love.

"Everything will be ok," she said.

"I know," he replied.

"The House of Mallory must not fall," she said, repeating what his father had told him. But her eyes were different than his father's. They were like her mother's, and they danced back and forth as she looked at one of his eyes and then the next. "We'll make sure of it."

He nodded and patted her arm as he descended the stairs to his chambers.

THE RULE OF THREE

ASHTON PULLED THE man off the cart and away from the fire and the arrows at Mallory Keep. He pulled with every muscle fiber he had available, and then pushed the corpse he feared to name onto his horse. He slapped it hard on the rear to get it moving and yanked on the gelding's reins.

The horse cantered slowly at first, but within a dozen steps or so, he realized Ashton's panic and galloped ahead of him. Ashton held onto the reins for as long as he could, running as fast as his legs could carry him. When his calves inevitably failed him, he crashed to the ground, being dragged for twenty to thirty feet before the rope leads were ripped from his fingers.

He heard the thud of the body falling from the saddle as Ashton pushed himself to his knees and hands in the mud and grass.

"Father," he cried, the sound of the label bringing tears to the corners of his eyes. "No, no, no…"

He found renewed strength and crawled across the ground to the naked man whose body lay twisted awkwardly nearby. He rolled his father over. There were multiple knife wounds to his sternum. He counted at least five.

"How did she know?" he asked, afraid to name her as Mekadesh because he felt she may call on him. "What have they done to you?"

A horse approached from the south, away from the men and women banging against the walls of the castle. Ashton cradled his father and turned his head toward the dark knight. The paladin had his war hammer still on his back and did not appear threatening.

"He left us," Ashton explained to the man, as if he were a friend. "He left my mother and me in Perketh. I hadn't seen him since."

"I'm sorry for your loss," the man in black said. "Truly, I am. This world has known suffering for too long. I fear it has lost memory of what it once meant to be full of life and love. To embrace the daylight instead of fearing it. To hope for normalcy."

Ashton stared at his father's dirty face. An anger swelled inside of him. If Karl hadn't left his mother Margaret, both of them might still be alive. Before today, Ashton had sworn that he hated his father—that he wanted nothing further to do with Karl Jeraldson. But that was when Karl was indestructible to his son. That had all changed when Ashton found Karl defiled on that cart. He didn't know what to feel. All he could do was cry and wish it were not so.

"You bastard…" Ashton muttered as tears coursed down

his cheeks and lingered at his chin. "Why weren't we enough for you? Why'd you have to leave us and remarry in Dona?"

Another man emerged from the shadows of trees to the southeast. He moved familiarly, but it wasn't until he left the darkness and crept into the light that Ashton recognized him. He was the elf who almost attacked him near Perketh the day he found Riley burned in the square. The elf moved like a cat, and his hands crossed over two knives hanging from his belt.

Unlike the dark knight with the yellow star on his plate breastplate, the elf wore only tanned leathers and a dark cape. The knight recognized the elf and nodded to him. He removed his dark plate helmet, revealing a man in his thirties with dirty blond hair and a clean-shaven face. His features were strong and masculine.

"You know what he's going to do," the elf said. His tone held a fear in it and maybe a promise.

"I mean to dissuade him," the dark knight replied.

"Dissuade me from what?" Ashton asked, still crying onto his father.

"My name is Cedric," the knight said, turning back to Ashton. "I'm what the common folk might call a paladin, by trade. But paladin's a title I inherited from my father, and one that I detest. It is my great shame. Like you, I held him as he lay dying, stabbed in the chest. Like you, I had to let him go."

"He doesn't have to go," Ashton said. "I can bring him back."

"Yes, you can," Cedric admitted. "I have seen such miracles with my own eyes."

"Miracles?" Ashton asked.

He could hear the moans and cries of the people he had brought back. All along the walls of Mallory Keep, which loomed large above the trees, his army flailed at the masonry. Some of them burned, and yet, still pounded at the stone battlements until their final breaths. Even closer, his resurrected friend Clayton limped toward them, maybe fifty paces behind the elf.

None of these undead seemed like miracles. More like wraiths from the underworld meant only for vengeance.

"This man," Cedric said. "Your father. He hasn't breathed for many days. He's dead. Gone. The Rule of Three. It must be respected."

"I don't know what you're talking about," Ashton said.

His friend Clayton passed the elf, and the dark assassin moved aside, retreating toward the forest a few yards. The elf watched Clayton warily.

Cedric knelt and inched toward Ashton, again trying to appear as non-threatening as possible. The necromancer instinctively drew his father closer. He knew that this paladin would take Karl away if he could. Cedric laid his massive war hammer on the ground.

"I'm not here to hurt you," Cedric said. "I don't fight in human wars. I don't get involved in petty squabbles. I'm here because you're here. I just want to make sure darkness does not pour into this land. I know many things—things that may help you."

Ashton bit his lip as the last of his tears pooled at his chin. Clayton limped past the paladin and drew near to Ashton's side.

"What's the Rule of Three?" Ashton asked.

"The spirit does not linger over a body long," the elf called from far away.

"I'll handle this," Cedric said firmly.

The paladin softened his tone and eyes toward Ashton. "How did you come to learn this gift?"

Clayton grunted and crossed his arms.

"I don't think they mean me harm," Ashton replied to his friend. "Well, maybe the elf does."

"Did you have a master?" Cedric asked.

Ashton thought of his master Nathan and nodded.

"Yes," he replied. He motioned toward Clayton inclusively. "We both did."

"And this man, your master, he didn't teach you about the Rule of Three?"

Ashton shook his head. He looked up at Clayton, but his friend was similarly confused.

"You're wasting time," the elf said. "Kill the both of them and let the armies of Mallory put down the rabble. They're already dropping pitch. It's only a matter of time before this horde is drowned in fire."

Clayton pounded a fist into an open palm.

"Ohhhh," the elf replied testily. "You think you have what it takes to rip me limb from stern? I've seen your lot. I've seen thousands of your lot, but I'm still standing. Fought you down to the dens of the underworld, and here I stand, breathing. You take another step forward, you cretin, and I'll end you!"

Ashton grabbed onto Clayton's pants, and yanked him backward.

"Your father's dead, friend," Cedric interrupted as he took a few small steps forward and knelt again. "Leave him in peace."

Ashton shook his head and crawled backward, pulling his father with him.

"OK," the paladin said. "OK. I'll stay right here. You have my word."

"End them," the elf said. "End them now or I'll do it."

"What are you so afraid of?" Ashton asked. "All we want is vengeance. Don't we deserve vengeance?"

He pointed toward the holes in his father's chest. "My father was many things. He was a drunkard. He was a malcontent. He beat me and my mother. He was gone for months at a time on his adventures to the north—times when my mother and I needed him. For a long time, we were glad to see him go, but even in his worst times, I never wished this…"

He ran his hand along the most deviated wound. "No one deserves this."

"No," Cedric said. "Of course not…"

"We all have it coming," the dark elf said. "Cedric here has his reasons. My people and I have mine. Your father? It sounds like he had more reason than most…"

"What's wrong with you?" Ashton asked, still holding onto Clayton's leg as his oldest friend made renewed efforts to smash the elf's face in. "Every time you open your mouth, malice drips from your gums.

"There was a time," Cedric said, "when Prince Jayden here was rumored to have a silvery tongue. He practiced it in great halls and wooed ladies by the hundreds. A poet long ago, were you not?"

"Those days are long gone," the elf said. "I haven't sung a flowery verse in a lifetime. I only carve words into the chests of the damned now."

"Are you saying I'm damned?" Ashton asked, still clutching his father and Clayton. "Or are you speaking of my father?"

"We're all damned," Jayden said, a sardonic smile creasing his lips.

"Then what's the harm in bringing my father back?" Ashton asked. "Why not give him a chance at retribution? Should he not be allowed to give these bandits chase to the ends of the world?"

"The ends of the world," Cedric said. "That's a curious thing to bring up right now."

"What're you talking about?" Ashton asked, angrily wiping tears from his face. "What are either of you talking about?"

"Where I'm from," Cedric said, "where I took my training, they have many books. Ancient things. Some are so brittle that they would crumble in but a breath from hurried lips. In them is old knowledge. Some would say forbidden."

"*Most* would say forbidden," the dark elf said. "They're literally outlawed in your own kingdom."

"*Anyway*," Cedric continued. "In one of these books is detailed the Rule of Three…"

"Is that one of *her* books?" Prince Jayden asked.

"Stay out of this!" Cedric warned.

"Get on with it," the dark elf said. "I can already see you've lost this argument. It's plain as day on his face."

Cedric waved Jayden off and looked intently and empathetically at Ashton.

"What's your name?" Cedric asked.

Ashton looked up at Clayton, who had fixed his legs in place, no longer trying to get to the elf. He instead listened intently.

"Why does everyone want to know my name?" Ashton asked. "The woman in Dona, the Mallories and now you?"

"I ask it only so that we might speak as friends," Cedric said.

Ashton sighed and removed his hand from Clayton so that he might cradle his late, absent father.

"They call me Ashton," he said. "Ashton Jeraldson."

"A good name," Cedric said. "Since you have given full weight of your friendship, I must give mine too. My last name is Errington. Cedric Errington."

The dark elven prince scoffed as he sat on his haunches near the edge of the clearing.

"This is all a waste of time," he complained.

"Ashton," Cedric said, "your father is gone. Surely, you can feel that, right?"

"Feel what?" Ashton asked.

"I've watched you in Dona," Cedric said. "You hovered there over the dead, watching and listening. I believe you felt them: their spirits. They linger, especially if they are torn violently from their bodies. It's the shock of their deaths that confuses them so. Murders are the most likely to leave a spirit behind for a time. The soul is not prepared for its passing. It waits for its limbs to respond once more. It grieves, in a way. Do you understand?"

"Yeah," Ashton said, nodding. "I felt it first in Perketh, while I sat over my friend's grave."

He patted Clayton on the leg.

"A strong bond," Cedric said. "It can keep the spirit near the body for a long time. That's where the Rule of Three comes from."

"The Rule of Three?"

"Three days," Cedric said, motioning toward Clayton. "You have three days to find the soul and bring it back to its body. Do that and you get your friend here. He remembers you. He may even remember himself. A human soul in a human body. The same loyalty and thoughts, for the most part. The same person."

"But Clayton has been the same person for more than three days," Ashton said.

"He's talking about being dead for three days," the elven prince shouted. "If you leave them dead for more than three days, the spirit's gone!"

"After three days," Cedric said, "it may be something else that returns. Something darker. It won't be loyal. It may know you. It may know your fears and your desires. It will certainly know how to manipulate you. It may even turn on you."

"The Rule of Three is not a law of nature," Prince Jayden said. "It is merely a guideline. Souls have left far sooner."

"And stayed longer," Cedric said. "The rule is a means of precaution."

"It's a means to take over this world," Jayden said. "Necromancy is not to be trifled with!"

"What does any of this have to do with my father?" Ashton asked.

"Your father was in Dona, right?" Cedric asked.

"I believe so."

"The bandits, this Red Army, came through Dona some five to six days past. I've been tracking them and you, and your father was the plaything of their leader, a man they call The Archer. Each morning he woke and he made your father's corpse a pin cushion. You can see his marks there on your father's chest."

"What of it?" Ashton asked.

"So, your father's been dead for nearly a week," Jayden

interrupted rudely. "He's gone. Just like my father. Just like Cedric's. Put him down. Bury him if you like, but do not try bringing him back."

"Or what?" Ashton asked.

"You humans are all the same," Jayden complained. "Everything's about you. Your feelings. Your wealth. Your greed. Not a one of you know what it's like to sacrifice. The world doesn't owe you anything. Not answers. Not time. Not love or grief. It's not all about you!"

"Can you feel him?" Cedric asked, waving Jayden off.

"Feel who?" Ashton asked.

"Can you sense your father about you?"

Ashton closed his eyes and swayed in the breeze. He could feel the air moving around him. He could hear the branches of the topmost limbs in the trees blowing in the wind and the sound of Jayden's gloved hand on his dagger. He could smell the sweat on Cedric's brow and the decaying flesh under his father's skin. But he could not sense his father's spirit.

"I don't know," Ashton lied.

"You bring this man back," Cedric said, "and you risk bringing darkness."

"Can you protect me?" Ashton asked.

"Protect you?" Cedric asked.

"Paladins deal in holy magics, right?"

The dark elf prince laughed maliciously. He pointed at Cedric and collapsed to his haunches.

"Hold your tongue," the paladin said, pointing at Prince Jayden. He pulled at the neck area of his breastplate as he turned back to Ashton. "In a way, I guess. If it's a… certain kind of darkness…"

"This is dangerous, and you know it!" Jayden said.

"You and I both know what pours out of Xhonia," Cedric accused. "The cat's out of the bag. Your devices have failed. We're at the brink of annihilation. Perhaps, he's the one…"

"It's a new age," Jayden said. "He's simply the first of many. The death throes of our planet."

"Do not lose hope," Cedric begged him.

"My people prepared for 10,000 years," Jayden said, "and for the next 10,000 years, we watched our cities fall, one-by-one. It's hopeless. There are a hundred prophecies, and they're all lies. Most of them were planted by the very ones we seek to destroy."

"Then we have nothing to lose, I guess," Cedric said. He motioned to Ashton to proceed. "Go ahead, then. If you must meet the darkness, then do it now while we are here. If it's not your father… If it belongs to the dark lords, then I will see it killed."

Ashton licked his lips and then gnawed at his lower one. Clayton knelt down beside him and put his hands on his friend and Karl. The dark elf prince inched his way closer with blades partially exposed. The paladin returned to his war hammer and the helmet he had discarded nearby. Suitably armored, he leaned against his weapon.

Ashton stared at the golden emblem on the paladin's chest. From afar, he could not distinguish its features, but up close, he saw the design was not as symmetric as he thought. It was like a rising sun from the horizon, but it seemed wrong—like the star emerged from the ground and not from just behind it.

"Father," Ashton whispered. "Are you there?"

He waited but the corpse did not respond.

"If you seek vengeance, I ask for you to join us."

He closed his eyes again and reached out for a spirit.

In the forest were many creatures. Deer. Squirrels. Ants and grasshoppers. A bandit hiding in a hollowed out tree trunk. But Ashton did not feel his father.

In the tree where the bandit hid, there were grubs and termites. Ashton followed their presence down into the black dirt. Earthworms squirmed in the packed earth. Snakes and all manner of vermin. Decayed leaves, remnants of life. He reached farther and was reminded of his dreams of Riley. Her skull-like makeup. Her dark eyes. The sockets of a skeleton, long dead. Eyelids flickered and he fell backward into the grass and mud.

Ashton leaned against his elbows, as his father rolled away and then pivoted on the ground in front of Ashton in circles. His father's corpse screamed as it rose to its feet, and Clayton struck a fighter's pose.

"No, no, no!" Karl cried. "Spare my life, Great One!"

He raised his hands as if warding off a blow, but the paladin only crept forward, and the sardonic smile of the dark elf prince was long gone. Replaced instead with loathing.

"What's this?" Karl asked. "How am I…?"

He laughed as he appeared to recognize where he was.

"It's OK," Ashton said, reaching toward him.

"Don't touch him!" Jayden yelled, gripping his daggers. "It's not your father!"

"So strange…" a raspy voice rattled from Karl's mouth. "This body… I was fighting in the darkness. I was dying…"

His father Karl turned around, toward Ashton. Dark lines emanated from his skin like heat rising from black tar left in the sun.

"Who do you serve?" the paladin asked, his hands wrapped ominously around the hammer handle.

Karl panicked and hid behind Ashton and Clayton, who turned around confused.

"I serve him!" Karl cried, pointing at Ashton. "He's my master now!"

"Which master did you serve before?"

"You are *her* man, are you not?" Karl accused. "The Holy One!"

"Bite your tongue!" Cedric threatened.

Karl whimpered behind Ashton.

"Back off!" Ashton commanded the paladin. "You stop threatening my dad!"

"He's not your father, boy!" Jayden repeated, holding both of his knives ready to throw. "Get away from him and give me a clear shot!"

"I'm his!" Karl promised again. "Let me stay in this world! I don't want to go back! He'll send me against her once more, or he'll force me to die to the Prince. Either way, I'm dead! Let me stay here. I'll prove my worth, I swear!"

"This creature lies!" Cedric said. "Do not worry. I will smite him!"

He stepped toward Ashton and Karl.

"No!" Karl screamed. He dropped to his knees and held onto Ashton's hands. He pawed at Ashton's feet. "Ask and it will be done! Command me!"

The paladin stopped.

"You cannot trust this thing!" Cedric said. "Believe me, I know!"

"I'm the most trustworthy thing in this world!" Ashton's father pleaded. Black and red lines continued to rise from his body. "Just ask it of me, and I'll do it. Let me prove myself to you."

"You're not my father," Ashton said. "My father would never…"

"I can be so much more than your father," the corpse said. "I can be devoted to you. Where he left you, I will never leave your side. I'll never go to Xhonia. I have no interest in the underworld—"

"Your father went to Xhonia?" Jayden asked. "What was he doing there?"

"Stealing, he was!" the creature said. "I wouldn't steal from you, master! Never! I live only to serve. I swear it!"

"What did he steal?" Jayden asked. He cursed and handled his blades like he was about to throw them or just scream.

"The device," the creature said. "You know the one, young prince! The one that froze the entrance to this world."

"You son of a—" Jayden threatened as he lunged forward.

The creature hid behind Ashton again and pulled Ashton away from the elf and the paladin. Clayton placed himself in front of Ashton. Far behind the advancing man and elf, Mallory Keep's walls wept black tar and fire. Fresh screams rose from the undead of Perketh and Dona.

A knife whirled through the air and embedded in Clayton's shoulder. He pulled it out and threw it to the ground. The elven prince held another knife at the ready, circling to one flank as the paladin moved to the other.

Far away, a bugle screeched a sour note and then issued forth a monstrous call, rattling the very trees and stones along the path. The elf broke from his attack stance and backed away. The paladin also seemed to lose his nerve.

"The king's cavalry," Cedric said.

Even from miles away, the many hooves of the King's Guard shook the ground and made Ashton's stance uneasy and fragile. He fell forward, and the creature he had raised into his father's body groped at him, pulling him back up.

"Ixfrit is here," the creature said. "Ixfrit has master! Do these nasty men threaten you?"

Jayden and Cedric stumbled back along the path, trying to maintain their balance as the heavy cavalry charged not far past the tree line. Ashton and Clayton followed not too far behind, and the naked corpse was never out of reach. He made sure of it by holding on to Ashton's brown tunic and cloak.

They each hid behind a thick tree trunk and watched as the King's Guard charged along the field, stomping over bandits and undead alike. Flaming corpses ran headlong into the stampede and were flattened deep into the muck. Ashton cried as he watched women he had brought back for their vengeance, scream in agony as they watched the horses trample their resurrected children and husbands and their dreams of retribution. Dozens fell to hoofs and lances. Then hundreds. The undead trampled each other as they tried to escape.

"Do these nasty men threaten you?" Ixfrit whispered into his ear.

"The King's men kill us indiscriminately!" Ashton complained. "They undo all that I set out to accomplish! The Mallories stand upon this ivory tower, raining down tar and fire. They escape justice. They maim and murder. They let others rape and violate their own subjects. Where is our vengeance? All is lost!"

"Does master command me?" Ixfrit asked. "Let me prove myself to you! Let me punish these bad men!"

Ashton looked to Jayden and Cedric, but they paid no heed to Ashton, Clayton or Karl's corpse. They watched the cavalry's grisly work.

"Go!" Ashton said. "Make them stop slaughtering my people. Someone has to bring justice to the Mallories. Help us!"

A misshapen smile spread across his father's face. "Ixfrit is here. Ixfrit serves his master. The bad men shall pay!"

Ixfrit roared fiercely like a lion and leapt past Ashton and Clayton. He raced past the elf and paladin.

"What the—" Cedric screamed as he watched the naked man run by him.

"No!" Jayden screamed.

The corpse seemed to bulge and grow to twice its size as it bounded toward the 100 foot tall walls. Its skin split, revealing fire and smoke underneath. His father's face crackled and cleaved around the mouth and along the neck.

"What have you done?" Cedric exclaimed as he ran past Ashton, back toward the place where Ashton raised the creature into his father. Cedric put his fingers to his lips and let loose a shrill whistle. His white horse stomped out of the woods and the paladin leapt into the saddle in a single, fluid motion as the horse fell behind the still growing creature in his father's corpse.

Ashton could hear the creature screaming as it came close to the King's Guard.

"Ixfrit is here! Ixfrit will punish the bad men!"

A cadre of imposing knights broke from their ranks and charged at the approaching creature. It laughed as they collided, and its attack was fierce and wild. Its hands had become dark claws, and they sliced through metal like a knife through butter. Ixfrit bit into the visor of the lead charger, and then ran his fist through a line of three knights, shattering their lances with his shoulder and chest.

Ixfrit never slowed down as he ripped through the King's men. A large man with a fur cloak and silver armor reared his horse and brought his sword down on Ixfrit's face, but the skin simply peeled off, exposing the air to flame and smoke. The creature tore the man in two, flinging his upper half hundreds of feet into the air. The knights of Kingarth panicked and parted as the creature became more enflamed.

"Ixfrit is here!" it roared. "Ixfrit will punish the bad men!"

Cedric was the only knight to pursue the creature. He held his hammer high, and a white light grew around the shaft and pommel. Other knights fell in behind him.

The creature laughed as it hit the outer wall of Mallory Keep. Its massive fists cracked the stone and a molten mass, like metal melted in the smithy, poured out of the white stone. Within seconds, a twenty foot section of the impossibly thick wall was tumbling down behind the creature. It bounded through the rock and into the killing fields beyond. Arrows and tar rained down but with no effect.

The creature continued to tear into the walls, cracking and melting the stone in the inner bastion until this too began to crumble. Screams echoed across the field, and Ashton watched in horror and shock as a lone man tumbled from the top of the largest wall. His black-and-white robes billowed in the winds as he fell, slowly and inexorably to the packed ground below. The loud, crunchy thud of him impacting the earth turned Ashton's stomach.

"Master!" Ixfrit screamed in triumph as he circled like a champion boxer next to the ruined inner corner of the bastion, where the man had fallen. "I have punished the bad men!"

The knights behind Cedric had faltered at the carnage. They had pulled reins and gawked, but Cedric had charged forward. He still raised his hammer high. He was upon Ixfrit before any fear could register on his fiery face.

"In the name of the Holy One," Cedric proclaimed in a strong voice that carried unnaturally across the field. Cedric leapt from his horse and heaved his hammer in a great arc from behind him. "I smite thee back to the underworld!"

The light-infused hammer came down upon Ixfrit's head, and like a hammer through glass, it shattered the creature into a thousand fiery fragments. They rained down for several minutes like ash from a campfire, eventually reaching Prince Jayden, Ashton and Clayton at the edge of the forest in small, glittery shards. The King's Guard made room for the paladin as he retreated, with head low, past the broken outer wall.

"What just happened?" Ashton asked. He looked at the dark elf behind him, but Jayden just gawked at the crowd and the still crumbling sections of the high keep.

The knights encircled the dead, and the chatter of their discoveries reached Ashton as a confused cacophony. In the forests far to the west, the remnants of Ashton's undead army watched on in disbelief and shock. A litter was quickly prepared from the remains of the bandit wagon caravan for a man at the center of the knight formation. They lifted it high above the crowd, but it contained only the bottom half of a silver-plated knight. A small group of mounted men charged into the eastern forest to retrieve the rest of him.

"Make way," a captain yelled to the gathered men. "Make way for the body of Crown Prince Magnus!"

Ashton's knees grew weak, and he collapsed to the ground. He watched the platform move to the edge of the forest where a group of knights dragged the armored torso of Prince Magnus toward the approaching litter.

Jayden snuck up beside Ashton, and he thought he was about to die. Clayton stumbled backward toward them, looking between Ashton and the broken wall. Jayden squatted to Ashton's left instead of putting a knife between his shoulder blades.

"We should have stopped you," Jayden said. "I told Cedric. I told him."

Ashton could not speak. His shoulders slumped as he absorbed the shock of what he had done.

A few of the knights in the King's Guard eyed the elf and the necromancer warily, but they all gave a wide berth to Cedric as he mounted his white horse and trotted through their scattered group. Some of them saluted the paladin. Others spit at him. He paid none of them any mind.

As Cedric came closer to Ashton, the knights looked at Prince Jayden. None said a word, but their eyes were daggers.

"They already mistrusted my kind," Jayden said. "Now, they think I did this."

"We should get out of here," Cedric said.

"You don't think we should turn him over?" Jayden asked.

"They hate what they don't understand," Cedric said.

"He killed the next in line to the Surdel throne," Jayden said, smacking Ashton in the shoulder.

Ashton felt numb. He had no strength in his legs or arms until Clayton offered his hand. Ashton nodded and grabbed Clayton to pull himself up. Jayden rose from his squat beside him.

"A demon did this," Cedric said, surveying the damage for himself, "and we may need this necromancer. The Age of Tranquility is over. The demon age is near. Humanity cannot hide from this any longer."

Jayden shook his head and grumbled. He called over a horse, and Ashton gathered the reins to his own gelding.

"We need to go somewhere we're out of the way," Jayden said as he pulled along Cedric.

"I know just the place," the paladin replied, spurring his horse to a trot and heading northeast.

Jayden followed closely, and Ashton carried up the rear. His head was down, deep within the darkness of his hood, but his eyes watched the litter that carried two halves of a man who had been ripped apart. The platform with the purple robe and white furs vanished into a crowd of polished armor and angry men.

As Ashton entered the forest, not too far behind Jayden, his eyes focused on the hooves of the horse in front of him. His mind wandered back to different nightmares, of hands grasping him from the underworld. He had thought nothing could have been worse than Riley's revenge.

He was wrong. He was very wrong.

THE SON RISES

JULIAN MALLORY STARED into his stylish black armoire. His father had told him to pack his belongings and be ready to flee to the caverns should the undead break into the Keep. Julian already had one suitcase filled with leather travel clothes, soft and durable wool shirts, and changes of undergarments and socks.

Julian loved his father. He trusted his father's instructions and knew that he must follow his father's orders. But there was another part of him that glanced at the mounted white suit of armor in the corner of his bedroom and thought of disobeying Lord Janus one last time.

Outside, a ragtag army assailed his family's home. Had they been orcs, his father might have sent Julian out to greet them with sword and steel at the head of the house knights. To die fighting for your house was a glorious death, one worthy of accolades.

But he did not want to meet these undead in battle

because he was brave. He wanted to face the undead because he felt that his life ending now, at this moment, might be the only way to make his father proud of him and save his legacy. It was only a matter of time before Lord Janus found out about the relationship Julian had with his sister.

They had stopped being careful months ago. Julian worried that his sister had wanted for them to get caught—to put an end to their affair and declare it to their father. That's why she must have been so brazen in the carriage. Why she had begun rubbing on him in the hallways more and drew him into her room, even when their father was home.

Julian would rather die than see the look on his father's face when that realization happened. All it would have taken for Julian to leap from the ramparts that morning would have been that recognition—for Janus to have realized what was going on and voiced it. He would have taken the fall and been glad of it—to finally put an end to his own suffering.

Julian stopped pretending to follow his father's orders and instead walked over to his white suit of armor with the black accents. Julian ran his fingers along the painted vambraces and the black pauldrons that fastened to the dark cape that hung behind it. The rest of the armor was pure white and fitted to his toned frame. His father had commissioned the suit when Julian was only seventeen. It had already seen use in three major skirmishes.

Julian ran his hand along a slight gash in the side of the metal breastplate, a reminder of an orcish war axe. He had split the orc's head in two for the insult with his steel longsword. The other engagements he had participated in with this armor were routs. No other creature or man had assailed him save that orc.

He looked back at the suitcase in front of the bed and then leaned his head against the white helmet on the black wall mount.

"Better he didn't know," Julian whispered. "Let him see me ride into the horde. Let him know me only as a fearless, foolish son. Not as the thief of my sister's chastity…"

The floor and walls shook and Julian crashed into his suit of armor. A great cacophony boomed behind him, and light filled the room. He turned, half expecting a giant or the hand of god himself to have broken his walls, ready to pluck him from his contemplation and cast him down to the underworld.

But when he pushed himself from his armor, there was no great palm waiting for him. No fingers clutched at his robe. He covered his eyes with his hand as he adjusted to the violent assault of daylight.

The armoire was gone, fallen into the gaping hole in the wall and floor. A man screamed and a large object flew by the floor-to-ceiling hole. Black-and-white with dark hair like his own. Brown eyes met Julian's in that brief moment, and Julian knew it was his father.

"No!" Julian screamed as he grasped the crumbling stone wall and leaned out. "Someone help!"

He leaned out and held onto a terraced edge of the stone wall outside of his room.

"Help!" he pleaded to anyone who might be listening on the ground far below.

Sometimes, when people tell stories, they say that time slows down in an important moment. A few seconds stretch on and become minutes or hours. The witness has an eternity to record every detail of the moment—to make sure that the smallest minutia of facts, sounds and smells is kept for poster-ity. Julian wished he had felt that time dilation, but such was not the case in the death of his father. It happened too fast.

His father pawed upward, toward him. He screamed and then rolled in the wind so that Julian could not see his face. Julian heard the hard, wet thud of his father's body hitting the stones and earth below. He saw the jet of blood and the gnarled mess of Lord Janus's final resting place.

"No," Julian said. "It was supposed to be me…"

He felt himself pulled toward his father, like a weak but persistent gravity tugged at his chest, beckoning him to follow his father's plunge.

"Julian!" his sister shouted from behind him.

Julian inhaled sharply, and he realized that it was his first breath since he had seen his father's eyes passing the huge hole in his wall and floor. Jayna hung precariously from the wall, reaching toward him.

"Jayna!" he cried as he fought off whatever force had beckoned him forward. He pointed downward. "Father…"

Jayna looked down and lost her sense of balance. Julian scurried across the overhang and pushed against her as he caught her, forcing her to topple inwards back into his quarters. She turned on her hands and knees, tears streaming down her face.

"Julian!" she said. "I thought you had… I…"

"I'm fine," he said. "I only went out to get a better look."

She crawled across the floor and grabbed his dark locks with both hands before kissing him strongly. "I cannot lose you…"

"But father…" he said. "Lord Mallory…"

She let go of his hair and carefully edged her way to the forty foot gap in Julian's wall and demolished floor. He reached out with his hand, and braced against a strong section of stone with his other. She held it firmly and peered over the edge.

"Father's dead," she said simply. She turned toward Julian. "You are Lord Mallory now."

"I—"

"You can make whatever rules you want," Jayna said.

"Whatever rules I want?" Julian asked uneasily, completely oblivious to her meaning. He was still in shock. In his mind's eye, he could still see his father's blood stains on the walls and ground below.

Jayna pulled against his shoulder and herself to him. She felt so warm against his thin robe.

"His lands are now your lands," she said. "His power is now your power. His castle is now your castle."

She kissed him.

"Our father has just died," Julian said.

"And we are finally free!" she replied.

She ran her fingers down his face, and he involuntarily closed his eyes and sighed as her fingertips brushed his lips.

"Master!" a strange voice yelled triumphantly from below. "I have punished the bad men!"

Jayna let go of Julian as he rushed to the edge. A strange man who seemed to emanate darkness and fire from large gashes and cracks in his skin was twirling in circles a few dozen feet below, his arms raised high above him. His fists appeared to melt as fiery tornados fought against the air near him.

A horse galloped toward the dark creature. The rider was painted black in his armor, and a small golden emblem of a star rising above a horizon jostled on his chest. The man was standing in his stirrups, a large war hammer raised high.

"In the name of the Holy One," the knight on horseback

shouted from fifty or sixty feet below. The rider bent his knees and vaulted himself forward as the horse wheeled to the side. The jettisoned man flew onward, the large, glowing hammer still in hand.

"I smite thee back to the underworld!" the knight yelled.

Julian watched as the dark figure with the tornados coming out of his body shattered into a thousand pieces and fire rolled out of him and over his father's body and white and black cape. The shards whirled violently in the wind, some of them reaching up to the perch where Julian and Jayna watched in horror.

Through the cinders, Julian saw his father's body catch fire and smolder.

The knight, undoubtedly a fabled paladin, spat at the ground where the creature had disintegrated before kneeling before Janus's body, crossing his chest with an extended hand, and offering a silent prayer. Julian immediately liked the black-clad man.

"I can fight bandits," Julian said, "and I can fight orcs. But how am I supposed to fight fiery creatures that destroy stone walls with their bare hands?"

Jayna shrugged her shoulders and shook her head. She then pointed down at the dark knight. "How does he?"

A commotion broke the paladin from his prayer and Julian from his contemplation. A line of carnage ran through the assembled men that extended from the forest all the way to the wall. A knight, who Julian immediately recognized as Lord General Godfrey Ross, held the bottom half of a man. The captain wept, and wails were going up around the battle-hardened knights below.

"Put on your armor," Jayna said in hushed tone. "Put on

your armor and make yourself presentable. We must hurry to the battlefield. What we do next is important! How the men see you next is important!"

"I must go bury father," Julian said, feeling suddenly weak with grief.

She pounded a fist against his chest, and he gave her a stern look as he rubbed his muscles.

"You are Lord Mallory now," she reminded him. "Not him. You must exert yourself immediately, while the fires are hot and the men are looking for leaders. Do not let someone else fill this void."

Julian nodded and grimaced as he scurried to his feet and removed his breastplate, cuisse, and greaves from the mount. Jayna grabbed a leather vest and pants from the suitcase that still sat on the floor in front of Julian's bed and threw them to him. He stripped his robe and put the leather garments on before slipping into his lower armor and then motioning for her to help him with his breastplate.

"Make way," General Ross yelled from the ground through Lord Mallory's destroyed wall. "Make way for the body of Crown Prince Magnus!"

THE DARK BROTHERHOOD

ASHTON STUMBLED THROUGH the dirty streets of Hell's Edge, a small town northeast of Mallory Keep, with his undead friend Clayton in tow. Before Ashton, the dark paladin and elven prince soldiered ahead, warily looking for threats, food and shelter. Hell's Edge was a town of adventurers and bandits and the last bastion of human civilization between the Kingdom of Surdel and the orcish hordes to the southeast. The town was poorly funded and guarded only by its inhabitants, the men and women crazy enough to live this close to certain death.

Ashton didn't know what had happened to his undead army. He only knew that they had served their intended purpose. The Red Army was destroyed. Lord Mallory, the man who had sat in his castle and allowed thousands of his people to die to a ragtag bandit army, was dead. There were no more targets to kill, and after raising a demon accidentally, Ashton had no intention of replicating his mistakes. He was the first to admit that he had no idea what he was doing anymore.

He had released something truly awful into the world. He promised himself that he would never raise another undead thing again.

Other than Clayton, his only companions over the past three days had been the silent dark paladin Cedric Arrington and the equally quiet Prince Jayden of the dark elves. The four men had quickly and quietly escaped from the field of battle.

There was no need for commands or consensus. They had not stayed to watch Prince Magnus being loaded onto a cart and taken back to the capital of Kingarth. There was no need for an "I told you so" from Jayden. There was no joyful boasting from Cedric about being the only person capable of sending the demon inside Ashton's father back to the underworld. They all knew they just had to get out of there, and Clayton simply followed Ashton wherever he went.

In Cedric's eyes, Ashton saw only pain and weariness. Jayden's eyes were harder to gauge. There was a sense of exhaustion there that was unfathomably deep. When the Prince stared at Ashton next to a fire, it was like looking into a bottomless hole in the earth. The Prince was completely unkept. His shockingly white hair fell down to his chest and back in loose, knotted locks that were held together with sweat and neglect. Everyone was similarly the worse-for-wear, but the Prince seemed even more affected by depression and exhaustion than Cedric or Ashton.

Ashton followed the two others because he had nowhere else to go. He followed them because he knew they must have more answers than he did. Even if they could only tell him more about what he had unleashed into the world, it was worth enduring the silence and the exhaustion. He felt he didn't deserve to be able to talk to people anyway. He needed to atone for what he had done in accidentally killing a celebrated, famous prince of Surdel.

The dark paladin and the dark elven prince stopped in front of an inn called "The Sleeping Pony." On its swinging sign were the trade guild emblems for food, drink and hoteling. The men didn't speak. They dismounted quickly and tied their mounts to a long wooden post on the side of the building. Cedric motioned with his head toward the door and then stomped through the threshold with his noisy plate armor. Jayden waited for Ashton to dismount and tie off his gray horse.

Ashton nodded toward his friend Clayton, who he knew would not follow him into a tightly packed room of people. Ashton wondered if Clayton too felt he needed to atone—that he didn't belong to humanity due to the nature of what he had become. Ashton placed a hand on his friend's shoulder.

"You waiting in an alley for me?"

Clayton nodded. Ashton saw the tell-tale signs of an assuring smile through the cloth that wrapped around the wounds on his face. Clayton limped away, and Ashton turned around to find the elf still standing at the doorway. He wasn't looking at Ashton though. His eyes darted between a small gathering of men leaning against a clay and straw building a dozen doors down and the retreating Clayton.

"Everything ok?" Ashton asked. The cacophony of the main hall of The Sleeping Pony grew louder as he approached.

The elf's white eyebrows raised, and he cleared his throat. Ashton realized that perhaps this simple question had been the first and only thing Ashton had said since his father's corpse had ran through the King's Guard.

"We're being followed," Jayden said.

"By who?"

"Two men," Jayden said, "and I think they're being followed by another."

The dark elf opened the door by a wooden handle, grabbed Ashton by his soiled hood and robe and shoved him through the portal. The main hall was packed to the walls with men in various stages of drunkenness. Ashton stepped over four passed out men, face first in the foul smelling floor rushes, as he caught up with Cedric at the main counter. There were at least five dozen men in a place that only sat twenty to thirty.

Cedric was leaning against the bar, conversing with the barkeep. The bartender had loose black curls and a clean-shaven face. He wore a light brown tunic that covered his rotund belly and a matching loose jacket and pants.

"I don't care how well I know you, Cedric," the barman said loudly, "and I don't care how much coin you've got. If you smell like you do, you need to go wash. Them's the rules. You damned well know it!"

"Harold, I just need something to drink," Cedric said. "Something strong."

"And you can have it," Harold said. "After your body soaks up some soap and water in a bath barrel. They're already preheated. You'll be back here before you know it."

"I'll need barrels for three then," Cedric said as Ashton stepped forward.

"What in God's name have you three been doing?" Harold asked, eying Ashton's soiled clothing and Jayden's matted hair.

"Lover's quarrel in the mud? Or were you actually fighting on the front?"

"The Red Army," Jayden said, casting Ashton a warning glance that clearly told him to keep quiet and let Cedric and Jayden do the talking.

"Ah," Harold said, "then you'll be celebrities once you get cleaned up. They say the Crown Prince has been murdered, along with that bastard Lord Mallory. Shame about the Prince."

"Aye," Cedric said simply.

"Shame," Jayden agreed.

"Been a bunch of posters put up around town," Harold said, looking at Ashton briefly as he cleaned a wooden mug.

"Posters?" Jayden asked.

"Big reward for this necromancer," Harold said, pointing toward posters on the wall at the end of the bar.

Ashton and Jayden drew near. There were two different versions.

The first notice had a rather dramatic rendering of a man with a flaring cloak and staff with a goat head on it. *Necromancer. Charged with the death of Prince Magnus, Lord Mallory, and hundreds of King's Guard at Mallory Keep. Thousands more potentially killed in Perketh and Dona. Wanted dead or alive.*

This poster was newer and overlapped an older one. The older one had a picture of a simple man in a cloak, a man not all that different from Ashton but with no discernible facial features under a dark hood in the engraving. *Supposed Necromancer. Wanted Alive for Questioning. Do not approach. Inform General Ross of the King's Guard.*

"I see," Jayden said.

Cedric, who had never left his leaning position near

Harold, held his helmet in the crook of his arm. He wiped his matted dirty blond hair from his face and stroked his stubbly chin and cheek.

"Can you send up your barber after you've drawn baths?" Cedric asked.

"The new man is good with a novacila and pumice," Harold said.

"What happened to Gerald? That pumice is such a pain. Plucking and pulling. Give me a copper razor any day."

"Oh sure!" Harold said sarcastically. "Maybe I should call for a depilatory cream. Mix together some of that readily available arsenic and our copious supply of quicklime and starch."

"A razor will do," Cedric said, raising his eyebrows and grinning slightly for the first time in days.

"Gerald's dead," Harold said simply. "Some type of plague."

"Speaking of which," Jayden said, sweeping the floor with a foot to reveal an older layer of reeds. "You should clean out these rushes. There's no telling what diseases thrive here."

"Why clean it out," Harold said, "when you can just lay down a new coat. Besides, the beer, piss and vomit soaks down to the floorboards. You would need to take a pick axe and a shovel to it to remove it."

"Or just drop a lantern on it," Jayden said, "and let the fire clean it once and for all."

Harold grunted and attacked another mug with the same rag.

"There's plenty of other bars and inns in town," Harold said. "I know you know them, because we barkeeps talk, and you've been kicked out of all of 'em."

"I'm sure the new guy will be fine," Cedric said, rolling his eyes. "Which room?"

"Eleven," Harold yelled a couple of times as a fight broke out near the doorway. "Get the hell outside with that!"

The combatants eventually obliged, and Harold shook his head as he cleaned another wooden mug.

"What type of ale do you have today?" Jayden asked.

"You can't drink down here until you've washed up," Harold reminded him. "You guys are going to run off all the customers."

"I'm asking for later," Jayden said, licking his lips.

"Roasted pale malt," Harold said, "until it's amber. Dark. Oats. Yeast."

"So, it's the strong mix then?" Jayden asked.

"Of course," Harold said, mocking outrage at any other suggestion. "I have to test each batch, and I won't be found dead sipping a weak cup. You want weak, you head down to The Fat Orc's Wife or The Slippery Eel."

Jayden smiled. "I thought you said we weren't allowed back into them. Kicked out, you said."

"Anyone would kick you out," Harold replied, "with the way you lot smell right now!"

Jayden raised his white eyebrows and hands and looked to Ashton with mock defeat. "Eleven, then?"

"Eleven," Harold said firmly, cleaning another glass and then the counter where an unruly, happy customer was sloshing around his drink as he sang a bawdy tune about a lusty midwife.

Cedric led the way up the stairs, helmet still in hand and a black cloak dragging along the steps. Ashton avoided the cloth. They entered a long hallway. Cedric expertly turned right without looking at any of the signs and pushed in a door to the left. Ashton just caught the numerals for eleven as he passed through the opening.

Three bathing barrels had already been prepared. The floor was soaked through with water and a film was clearly visible from the layers of soap that had been spilled here. Ashton looked down at the cracks in the floor, expecting to see bar patrons, but instead there was just brown earth. The room was situated behind the bar, so the dirty water fell outside.

Jayden disrobed first, as he was less encumbered and certainly the least shy. He slipped into the central barrel. Cedric had problems getting rid of his armor, and Ashton, having some experience with such gear at the smithy, helped him undo the fastenings of his breastplate. Cedric took the wooden basin closest to the door. Ashton entered his bath last, the one closest to the only window in the upstairs room. The water had been boiled at some point in the past but not anytime recently. It was lukewarm, but for a person who had been traveling, it was like a thermal vent in the lap of luxury.

Ashton laid there for a few minutes, only moving to submerge his head in the soapy liquid and listening to the clamor from the nearby main hall carrying through the water.

After the third dunk, he noticed Jayden was looking at him. He leaned against the barrel and stared back, waiting for Jayden to have something to say.

"No one's going to understand what happened at Mallory Keep," Jayden said.

"I certainly don't," Ashton said, wincing as Jayden glared at him. He shut up after that.

"Just start from the beginning," Cedric said. "He's of no use to us ignorant. He's a piece of this puzzle. I'm sure of it."

Jayden twisted his mouth and then frowned before speaking again.

"We first came into contact with them 20,000 years ago," Jayden said. "The demons. There was a dark elf amongst us named Selenor. We didn't have restrictions on magic, but back then, there was nothing especially dangerous about wielding it. There were no necromancers. Only magicians. Selenor was a projector. Astral projection, they call the art. From our world, she would travel out into the stars, touching other worlds. She grew tired of the other local planets. All barren and lifeless. So, she ventured farther. My great grandfather told me she used to draw crowds—almost like parades—regaling the people with her adventures amongst the stars."

Cedric shook his head and dipped back briefly into the water, rubbing soap on his scalp as he came back up.

"She found an ancient being," Jayden said, "one of the oldest. At least, that's what this other woman claimed. Said she was a queen, that she had created whole races of creatures. That she could teach Selenor how to visit different planes of existence. That was the first we heard about the Abyss. The Void."

Jayden stared off into space for a few moments. The mumble and thuds of the muted crowd from the main hall seemed more pronounced as he focused his hearing. Ashton waited on baited breath.

"This creature," Jayden said, "this Queen. She was very interested in us. What we were working on. The magics we possessed. As part of a cultural exchange, we educated her. In return, she gave our world a name: Nirendia. She said she wanted to come here, to see our world. Our Council at the time agreed to it."

"Humans should have been included in that discussion," Cedric complained.

Jayden ran his hands through his white hair. He then leaned back to stare at the ceiling.

"We tried to prepare our world," he said. "We knew of certain magics that limited projection, allowed us to corral a creature like her into a certain space. We spread this magic over the world around Surdel. It took us thousands of years. The surface was covered with magic, and a natural cavern lined with the stuff exists under this land thanks to a long ago cataclysm."

"But you didn't seal the dark elven cities," Cedric added.

"Yes," Jayden said. "Back then, the humans didn't have cities. Ours was the dominant population. We ruled the land. Even the eastern wood elves bowed to our dominion. We thought our cities were strong because our people were strong and wise. We were idiots. This Queen came to this world about 15,000 years ago. We met her below Balahambria. It was a great city back then. Lots of history and magic. All lost to time and demons."

"You doomed us all," Cedric accused mildly, and Ashton realized these two men had had this same conversation many times. Cedric was just going through the motions.

"I wasn't alive back then," Jayden said. "I'm only 2,000 years old. My mother too was unborn then. Anyone involved in this *cultural exchange* is long dead. I'm as liable for what happened there as you are for the rise and fall of the paladins."

Cedric grunted and lowered himself into the barrel so that only his nose and parts of his face were exposed above the cold water.

"Anyway, Balahambria was the first to fall," Jayden said.

"We found out what she really was then, as best anyone can figure out what she is. She's false. She lies, but of one thing we're certain: she's a demon lord."

"What's a demon lord?" Ashton said.

"I can't tell you what defines it," Jayden said. "She boasted of many things. Her conquests. Her creations. She claimed that she created the modern form of demons. Before her, they were more ethereal. Dark creatures. She gave them the claws, the fire, and the form."

"What does she look like?" Ashton asked. "I met a woman, a dark goddess, in Dona."

"What was her name?" Jayden asked.

"That's what I kept asking her," Ashton said, "and she wouldn't answer."

Jayden sighed. "So, she didn't tell you…"

Cedric popped back up from his barrel.

"She told me a name," Ashton said. "She claimed it was the name that the Prince of Demons used for her. She claimed she had created creatures called naurun. She claimed she had raised that Prince of Demons from these very demons she had created."

"Fire creatures," Jayden said. "Naurun means fire creature. That's what you raised from your father at Mallory Keep. You raised one of the creatures she helped spawn."

"So, you *have* met her?" Cedric asked, running his hands through his dirty blond hair and leaving his palms in his eye sockets.

Ashton nodded, his chin splashing against in the water.

"What did she have you call her?" Jayden asked.

"Mekadesh," Ashton said. He looked around expecting

her to appear, but she did not. "She said the Prince of Demons calls her Mekadesh."

Jayden exchanged a mirthful look at Cedric, who submerged back into his barrel. Jayden chuckled briefly and then turned back to Ashton.

"That's a more recent name," Jayden said. "Still ancient but not the first. As I told you, when she first came to my people, she told us that her people, the durun, called her Queen."

"But queen is a title," Ashton said.

"For her, it was a name," Jayden said, "or maybe she was the first queen to have ever been. Regardless, she wanted us to call her that. It was unlikely to have been her first, but her birth name may be lost to time. We know her people call her the Queen of Chaos."

"Her people," Cedric scoffed. "You mean the demons you've captured and tortured?"

"You have fondness for them?" Jayden asked.

"No," Cedric said defensively.

"Of course you do," Jayden said. "After all, you can't kill them can you? You know why that is. You're not dumb, even if you're under her spell."

"Watch your tongue," Cedric warned from his barrel. His eyes were dangerous.

"Her people could be numerous," Jayden said. "These durun, who I've never seen, are said to be her original people. She created the naurun, but they're not all her people. The demon lords we know about came from them, and they each lead factions of the fire creatures. She claims to have made other creatures."

"She boasted to me that she had as well," Ashton said.

"She claimed that she's a champion of nature. She told me that she's even made creatures on our world."

Jayden shared a meaningful look with Cedric, but Ashton had no idea what transpired. Cedric shook his head adamantly.

"You and I both know the truth about the Holy One," Jayden said.

"The truth is that I fight demons when other men cannot," Cedric said. "The truth is that I've done plenty of good. I've sent many naurun to the Void."

"There's no point arguing with you about this," Jayden said. "I know you cannot change the past, and you won't even speak to it. My people do not fight the Queen now. We fight Orcus who retreats from Demogorgon, the Prince of Demons. You and your people can still make a difference at Uxmal. The demon lords are each looking for a path to the surface. They would make our world a furnace and crust over the land with new conduits to attack each other and Mekadesh."

"What do they want?" Ashton asked.

"Their reasons are their own," Cedric said, squirming with discomfort in his cooling bath. "Who knows why they do what they do?"

"Some fight for dominion," Jayden said. "Demogorgon fights the other demon lords to establish his dominance. The naurun we've questioned say he's never lost a plane of existence."

"A plane of existence?" Ashton asked.

"From what I understand," Jayden said, "demon lords fight for control of what they call a level of the Abyss. Each level was once a world like ours, and once it was conquered, it merged into the Abyss as one of these lairs or planes of existence. The demons we've captured claim that Demogorgon has the most planes under his control. They say he is so powerful that he can hypnotize other demon lords into subservience by simply gazing at them with his two heads."

"Is that true?" Ashton asked.

"No idea," Jayden replied.

"He has two heads?" Ashton asked.

"That's what they say," Jayden said.

"You can never trust a demon," Cedric said, his voice dripping with melancholy. "If you heard this from a demon, you've probably been misled."

Jayden laid a hand on Cedric's shoulder. He patted the paladin and then withdrew his hand.

"So, you've never seen this Demogorgon?" Ashton asked.

"No," Jayden said.

"Nor I," Cedric said.

"Who is Orcus?" Ashton asked.

"A rival of Demogorgon," Cedric said. "Lord of the Undead. A chief rival to the Prince of Demons."

"He raises people from the dead?" Ashton asked. "Like I do?"

"Your power's source is undoubtedly due to his presence in our realm," Cedric said, "but he certainly doesn't just raise people. The dead simply respond to him wherever he goes. They rise up without him saying a word."

Jayden nodded in agreement. "We fought many of our own kind in the caverns of Chejit and Daydira."

Ashton's heart sank. He wanted nothing to do with demons. He had seen enough of their work at Mallory Keep. His power couldn't have come from Orcus.

"But you don't know that for sure!" Ashton said, pleading with Jayden.

"In the thousands of years we studied magic before they arrived," Jayden said, "not one case of necromancy had been reported in any kingdom of Nirendia. Orcus came and the undead were everywhere underground. It's unlikely to be a coincidence."

Ashton gnawed at his lip, trying to twist the source of his power in his mind.

"But that doesn't mean anything, does it?" Ashton asked. "I didn't ask for these powers. So what if they come from a demon? If I help people with them, can I not still use them? For good?"

Cedric stared ahead, and Jayden looked at the paladin. Again, Ashton felt something unspoken was passing between them. He felt like this awkward silence had a long history between these two people.

"Can I give this power back?" Ashton asked. "I don't want it."

"A demon's power always has a cost," Cedric said, "and not so easily undone."

"Am I a demon?" Ashton asked.

"Are you a demon?" Cedric repeated. He turned to Ashton with confusion on his face.

"If I'm empowered by a demon," Ashton said, "then what separates me from them?"

"They put a darkness on our souls," Cedric said. "Maybe you have a darkness. Maybe not."

"Are you going to smite me?" Ashton asked, looking at the paladin's hammer in the far corner next to the door. "To remove the darkness placed on my soul?"

Cedric laughed involuntarily. "No, boy. You're not a demon. You're just a man."

Ashton breathed a sigh of relief. "So, what does this Orcus want with me?"

"Maybe nothing," Jayden said. "Your power may have been accidentally bestowed. Orcus wars with Demogorgon in the underworld. The undead swarm the naurun. The naurun swarm the undead, and somewhere out there, Mekadesh may even field her durun against the both of them. On and on the battle wages beneath us, and we are powerless to stop it."

"And sometimes, it spills out," Cedric said, "and that's where you'll find what remains of the paladins."

"And the dark elves," Jayden said.

The pair stopped talking as the creaking of foreign footsteps approached outside the door. The paladin left the water and carefully crossed the floor to his weapon without making a sound. He stood there, naked as a newborn, deadly and ready to strike whoever entered. A knock came on the door, and Cedric poised his war hammer for a swing.

"It's Harold," the familiar voice said through the door. "Are you decent?"

The paladin gently placed his weapon back into the corner and retreated to his tub.

"Never," Cedric said as he slipped back into the cold water.

The door opened and Harold smiled above a tray of three wooden mugs.

"You're a saint," Cedric said.

"In your order?" Harold asked mockingly. "No thanks!"

The paladin grabbed a mug and Harold offered the next one to Jayden. The elf raised the mug to Harold in thanks before gulping down the contents. Ashton took his mug last and held it between both hands.

"You sure this one is old enough to drink?" Harold asked, turning his head toward Cedric.

"I've seen you serve this swill to five-year-olds," the paladin replied.

"I only want to know if he can hold his alcohol," Harold said with jovial mirth. "I have enough to clean up downstairs already."

Harold looked at Ashton with rapt attention, apparently waiting for some witty remark—for Ashton to join in on the banter.

"Can I hold my liquor?" Ashton asked. "Is that what you're asking?"

Harold nodded.

"No," Ashton said with a straight face, "but I'll be sure to splash my vomit with a little bit of bath water."

The elf and paladin laughed.

"Maybe just put down another layer of rushes," Jayden said. "That's how Harold here cleans up all his messes!"

"Attaboy!" Harold said, slapping Ashton wetly on the shoulder after he pressed the empty tray between his arm and his chest. "Hey, don't expect any further room service like this, lads! You want more, you have to come downstairs!"

Cedric and Jayden raised their mugs. Ashton joined them but too late for Harold to see. Harold turned around and exited the room, closing the door behind him.

The three men silently drank their ale for a few minutes, letting the cool water soak into their skin.

"So, this Queen of Chaos," Ashton said, "this Mekadesh, she was the first demon lord to come to our world?"

"15,000 years ago," Jayden agreed. "Invited by the dark elf Selenor."

"And she took Balahambria, a dark elf city?"

"She tried," Jayden said. "We sealed the city with ice magic. Selenor told us that the naurun were creatures of fire. We tried to take precautions. We covered the land with ice magics for nearly a thousand years in preparation for the Queen's arrival to isolate her and seal her into the space beneath Surdel. The demon lords seek a path above the ground to flank and surprise their rivals. That's what our captives have told us. That's why they assault our dark elven cities. They are the only gateways to the surface."

"Where did she go next?" Ashton asked.

"She didn't go anywhere," Jayden said. "We didn't hear from her for thousands of years. Maybe she traveled back and forth between Nirendia and the Abyss. Maybe she left and only came back when she needed to."

"Why?" Ashton asked.

Jayden shrugged.

"Because the other demon lords arrived," Cedric said. "Orcus and then Demogorgon. That's what it says in our archives. She wasn't as interested in gaining a new plane like the others. She wants something else."

"She told me something similar," Ashton said. "She told me she was here looking for something that was hers. She mentioned something about a vision of a general guy named Maddox? I don't know what any of this means."

"She talked to you often?" Cedric asked.

"Just once in Dona," Ashton said. "I've just been thinking about it ever since, trying to understand it."

"I told you," Cedric said to Jayden. "The books are not lies."

"Well," Jayden said, "I guess you'd know best."

Cedric gave Jayden another warning glance over the top of his mug.

"I only mean that your archives would obviously be the more complete," Jayden said innocently. "Your connection to demons is stronger than mine."

Cedric growled.

"I have no intention of provoking you," Jayden said, "but if the boy wants answers, it's difficult to dance around these subjects just so you feel better. Perhaps you can tell him."

"You know I can't do that," Cedric said.

"Tell me what?" Ashton asked.

"It doesn't matter," Cedric said.

"The paladins entered the fray about 9,000 years ago," Jayden said. "They had a unique power over demons. Of all the magics we had ever studied, theirs was the most potent against the naurun. For 7,000 years, dark elves and paladins kept the undead and the naurun in check. We fought the demons in the caverns of Xhonia in the north and Shamat in the far northwest."

"Demogorgon took Shamat around 2,000 years ago," Cedric said. "Shamat was where we saw the first deathknights deployed. They rode up the caverns on a twisted type of horse they call nightmares. Jet black. Flames for manes. They moved quickly, and the undead men on top of them wielded green fire. Some type of fel energy. They're smarter than the naurun. Much smarter."

"Shamat fell within days," Jayden said. "We had to seal it quickly, freezing thousands of elves in the city and caverns."

"Orcus took the biggest prize," Cedric said.

"Ul Tyrion," Jayden said. "Our capital. Home to our main library and university. We lost everything. My father died there. All of my grandparents. My mother and I escaped, and the city was sealed behind us. We've been fighting ever since."

"He didn't hold it for long," Cedric said. "Demogorgon's deathknights came from the west, and they took the caverns under the city as fast as they had conquered Shamat."

"That all happened about 1,500 years ago," Jayden added. "Demogorgon and Orcus continued to fight for centuries without us knowing about it. The next catastrophe happened a thousand years later at Xhonia."

"What happened?" Ashton asked.

"We were betrayed," Jayden said.

"By whom?" Ashton asked.

Jayden looked at Cedric, whose face grew white as a sheet. The dark elf waited for the paladin to finish the story, but Cedric uttered not a single word.

"The paladins had no effect against The Queen of Chaos's forces," Jayden said. "In fact, they helped her. Turned on us. Many dark elves fell under their weapons. We sealed that city with an ice magic device and again lost thousands. The paladins fought us as we retreated, but as the city was sealed, they seemed to come to their senses. She lost her connection to them, and they broke free."

"The paladins were disbanded by the King," Cedric said simply. "We could not be trusted. We lost all land and titles. We couldn't even call ourselves knights. We scattered across the land."

Ashton began to understand the dark knight's melancholy.

"Phiol fell to Orcus a hundred years later," Jayden said. "He kept moving east, taking Chejit and Daydira. We sealed him in, and one-hundred-years-ago, Demogorgon overtook Phiol with naurun cavalry and deathknights. Fifty-years-ago,

Demogorgon pushed Orcus out from under Chejit, and the Demon Lord of the Undead retreated north from Daydira. We're not sure if Demogorgon is there yet. All we know is that he's winning."

"How many dark elven cities are left?" Ashton asked.

"Just one," Jayden said. "Uxmal to the far east."

"And once that is sealed," Ashton said, "the demons are trapped forever?"

"Who knows?" Cedric asked rhetorically. "We haven't seen everything they're capable of. We survive because they're distracted. Whether Uxmal falls or not is irrelevant. They know that when they finally turn their attention to us, we'll melt before them like wax to flame."

"Uxmal is not just an opening into this land," Jayden said. "It's the last remnants of my people. If it falls, my people are done."

"You should just seal it," Cedric said.

"Are you really the one to tell me what I should and should not do?" Jayden asked testily. "Besides, this one's father," he pointed at Ashton, "apparently unsealed Xhonia, took the device and allowed demons to potentially invade the surface a few years ago. What good is all of this sacrifice if one man can undo all of it? Perhaps this Karl character and his bandit friends have all of the devices. Hundreds of thousands of my people might have died for nothing."

Ashton felt a deep wave of shame flow over him. His father had always been an embarrassment. To think that Karl Jeraldson might have also damned the world was a bit too much. Ashton felt tears welling at the corner of his eye. He rubbed a fist against his face.

"I cannot answer for my father," Ashton said, "but if there

is a way to fix this, if there is anything I can do to help, then I'll do it."

"Xhonia is likely swarming with demons now," Jayden said. "We'd need to either retrieve the device or find a new one. Then, we'd need to fight our way down to a point that would actually seal the area around it. We can't just leave it outside the gates and hope for the best."

Ashton nodded. "Maybe I can raise an army to help us fight."

"And fight the demons and their undead with your undead?" Cedric asked.

"Yes."

"What's the point?" Cedric asked.

"We don't need to beat them, do we?" Ashton asked. "I mean, did the elves ever beat them?"

Jayden shook his head with disappointment. "We've only bought the rest of the world time."

"And that's all we need, right?" Ashton asked. "Just enough time to bring the device to where my father had taken it and then reactivate it."

Jayden shrugged. "Maybe. But let's say we succeed in sealing Xhonia again. The demons will just move on to Uxmal."

"What do you want to do?" Ashton asked. "Give up? We buy more time for your people. We stick to the plan."

"There is no plan," Jayden said. "There is only what the demon lords want and how long we can hold them off."

"Fine," Ashton said with frustration, "then what do the demons want? If we know what they want, maybe we can use that against them."

Cedric laughed. "Now, we're supposed to understand the

intentions of demons? Maybe they just want to kill us all and rule this world."

"Each demon lord wants something different," Jayden said.

"And you would know what they want?" Cedric asked.

"As much as they're willing to say," Jayden said, "and what their minions have revealed to us when pressed."

"And what were they *willing* to say?" Cedric asked.

"Orcus wants to be Prince of the Demons," Jayden said absently, staring into the door. "He needs to gain more planes of existence. Demogorgon wants to solidify his power further in the Abyss. The Queen of Chaos wants something different…"

"What does she want?" Ashton asked. "Does anyone know?"

"Maybe," Jayden said. He leaned back against his barrel and sighed.

"And?" Cedric asked.

"She came to me in a dream when I was young," Jayden said. "She was dark and beautiful and trapped under the world. I was engaged to my one true love at the time in Ul Tyrion. Mekadesh told me that my betrothed would die and that I would need a new dark princess. She told me I would be her next husband, and that we would create a new race of creatures the universe had never known. Dark and powerful and wielding all the magics my people had developed over the millennia. She promised me infinite power, and a spot by her side for all eternity."

Cedric's mouth was agape. Prince Jayden's description reminded Ashton of his dreams of Riley in the Underworld. He wondered if the Queen of Chaos had been playing with his mind too this whole time, before he had even met her in Dona. She hadn't promised him power or eternity. She may have simply been toying with him and enflaming his passions.

Then, she may have appeared to him at Dona to entice him into thinking about commanding her legions, to channel that passion for justice into leading her creatures.

The idea fit in his mind, but he didn't want to be part of her plan. He'd much rather Jayden be her true target.

"The Queen of Chaos," Ashton said, "is *here* for *you?*"

Jayden nodded slowly. "That's what she told me. She told me that she would kill my mother, and I would be King of Etyria. She would marry me, and she would be queen of yet another race of creatures. She told me that where she failed in leading the durun and creating the naurun, she would succeed with the dark elves. She told me I would smite her old lover Demogorgon and drive Orcus into the Abyss. I would roll through the other demon lords like a scythe through dry grain."

The three men quietly pruned in their wooden barrels. Ashton was the first to break their silence. He felt it was time to reveal her conversation in more detail.

"She told me she wanted me to be her general," Ashton said. "She wanted me to lead her legions of demons and raise a new army of undead against her enemies."

"That's not surprising," Cedric said. "She likes to twist your passions and powers into her own causes."

Jayden nodded. A smile spread across his face.

"As the potential next King of Chaos," he said with some pomp from his bath barrel, "I guess I do have need of a general. You know. A man I can trust to help me assault all the armies of the Abyss for my Queen."

Ashton nodded and shrugged his shoulders through the water. He smiled playfully to Jayden and his mock proposal. "I guess, if I have to."

"You guys are making me feel a lot better," Cedric said, leaning toward them. "She only wants me for my soul!"

The paladin grinned widely, and Jayden and Ashton both shared in the mirth. They burst into laughter, splashing each other with soiled, soapy water.

"Over my dead body!" Jayden said.

"And my hordes of undead ones!" Ashton promised.

After winding down their laughter, Cedric left his basin first. As the paladin dressed, Jayden and Ashton shared a look of respect.

"We'll find a way," Cedric promised as he opened the door. He nodded to them, closed the door, and walked noisily down the stairs to the main hall. "She won't win. None of them will."

Jayden dressed next in his soiled outfit.

"Probably should have washed those," Ashton said.

"Maybe tomorrow," Jayden said. "Tonight, I'm going to get drunk."

Ashton nodded, and Jayden left as the paladin had before.

Ashton stayed in his tub for a while longer. He thought about his dreams of Riley in the underworld, and the visit from the Queen of Chaos in Dona. He thought about the demon ripping through knights in front of Mallory Keep and melting through the foundations of a castle with his bare hands. He thought about his father running for his life from Xhonia, a mysterious device hidden in a bag. Then he remembered his undead friend Clayton waiting on him in some alleyway to finish his bath.

"I'm such an asshole!" he exclaimed.

He dressed quickly and ran down the stairs, leaving the door to the washroom wide open. He waved to Cedric and

Jayden at the bar, each raising a mug to him as he ran toward the front door. He pushed the door so hard that it slammed against the wall loudly.

"Sorry!" Ashton shouted back to the barkeep Harold. "My bad!"

He found his friend in a dark alleyway across the street, arms folded, sitting against a wooden building.

Clayton stood up and groaned something.

"I just came out to see you," Ashton said, grinning.

He put his arm around Clayton as they walked together into the darkness and the cold night. A strong smell of flowers wafted into his nose with every squeeze of his friend's torso, and with every retelling of old stories, he found himself pulling Clayton closer to his side.

"I love you, man," Ashton said. "Thanks for being here with me."

Clayton groaned and mumbled something while shyly looking away.

"Well, I mean it," Ashton said.

Outside of The Sleeping Pony, Lord General Godfrey Ross waited in nondescript, ratty garb covering his plate armor. A gray hood draped down to his eyes as he leaned against a nearby wall in the darkness. Beside him, Jeremy Vossen, one of his son's closest friends, held a gloved hand over his long sword pommel. Jeremy too did not outwardly wear his house colors, and he had shaved his beard to be more incognito. A long length of rope wound around his arm.

"I need him alive," Godfrey reminded Jeremy. "Don't kill him."

"If he sends that undead brute after me," Jeremy said, "I may have no choice."

"If you kill him," Godfrey said, "then my son can't be brought back from the dead. He'll sit in that icebox back in Kingarth until I fetch him and put him into the ground. Is that what you want?"

Jeremy sighed deeply.

"If there's a way to bring my son back," Godfrey said, "then by all the gods, I'll…"

The door to The Sleeping Pony slammed loudly against the wooden wall, and a dark figure exited.

"Sorry!" a young man yelled. "My bad!"

"That's him!" Godfrey whispered to Jeremy.

Jeremy nodded to Godfrey and unwound the rope from his arm. He looped the rope into a lasso and tied a sliding knot that would tighten the more his target struggled.

"Follow him," Godfrey said. "I'll grab the horses."

THE END OF
THE PEOPLE'S NECROMANCER

Book One of the Age of Magic

The Age of Magic continues in

THE DARK
PALADIN!

THE AGE OF MAGIC SERIES

The People's Necromancer
The Dark Paladin
The Dragon Prince
The Red Poet
The Queen's Consort
The Blood Chief
The Holy One

About the Author

Rex Jameson is the USA Today Bestselling author of the Primal Patterns series, the Age of Magic series, and half a dozen short stories. An avid history buff and an unabashed nerd with an appetite for science fiction and fantasy, he loves to create complex speculative fiction with layered characters. He earned a PhD in Computer Science at Vanderbilt University and researches distributed artificial intelligence in robotics at Carnegie Mellon University. Rex and his wife Jenny live in Pittsburgh where they enjoy hosting family and friends.

OTHER FICTION BY REX JAMESON

The Primal Patterns Series
Lucifer's Odyssey
The Goblin Rebellion
Shadows of our Fathers

The Perspectives Series
Angels and Demons: Violent Afterlife
Elves and Goblins: Father's Rebellion

Other Fiction
Hallow's Ween
"Don't Mess with the Meadow" in the Pink Snowbunnies Ski
in Hell Anthology.
"Saving Suzanna" in The Pride Collection.

If you liked this book and would like the series to continue, please be sure to leave a review on Amazon.com, BarnesAnd-Noble.com, GoodReads.com, and other places where readers congregate. Also, tell your friends!

Author website: http://www.rex-jameson.com
Newsletter: https://rex-jameson.com/new-releases-email-list

Made in the USA
Las Vegas, NV
17 December 2021

38445929R00142